THE SCOTCH KING

BOOK ONE

PENELOPE SKY

Hartwick Publishing

The Scotch King

Editing Services provided by Final-Edits.com

CREWE

Handcuffed and sporting a black eye, Joseph Ingram sat in the black chair with his hands bound behind his back. The left side of his lip was swollen from a powerful fist, and his tailored suit possessed holes from the burning end of a cigarette. Two of his men flanked him on either side, just as bloodied as he was.

Stirling Castle was so ancient my mind couldn't comprehend it. Built in the 12th century, my Scottish ancestors lived in luxury. Times had changed, but the family line had remained intact. I was the owner of this fine landmark, but its sole purpose was for business endeavors.

Like this one.

I entered the room in my black suit with matching black tie. My silver cufflinks caught the dim light as I took my seat across the table from Joseph, a man I despised immensely. When it came to business, personal opinion was irrelevant. Whoever paid the right price was entitled to whatever I had to offer.

But this man made the mistake of betraying me.

He couldn't meet my gaze, afraid of my wrath. Foolish for thinking he would get away with it, he was now at my mercy. I could do anything I wanted, and he knew it. I could kill him and bury him in the graveyard where my ancient ancestors rotted. I could cut up his body and drop the pieces off the coast.

Joseph bowed his head slightly, as if the muscles of his neck couldn't keep his head upright. He reminded me of a baby, too weak to carry his own weight.

I crossed my legs under the table and unbuttoned the front of my suit. One hand rested on my propped-up knee as I examined my foe, this idiot with an ego too big to handle. I traded him some valuable intelligence for a premium price—four million dollars.

But he didn't pay up.

Instead, he gave me counterfeit bills.

Like I wouldn't have figured it out. "You insulted me, Joseph."

The second I spoke, he flinched slightly. He adjusted his body in the chair, and no matter how much he tried to hide it, he shook. I spotted the tremble in his arms, the shake of his extremities.

"And you know what I do to people who insult me."

He cleared his throat, his Adam's apple moving as he swallowed. "Crewe—"

"Mr. Donoghue." Dunbar was my right-hand man, serving out his life in voluntary servitude. I saved his life and gave him the vengeance he deserved. As a result, he devoted his life to serving me—loyally.

Joseph cringed at the false move. "Mr. Donoghue, I'm sorry."

I chuckled because he was making it worse. "Don't apologize. Men like us don't apologize for our wrongdoings. We have every intent of lying, stealing, and misleading our victims. Own up to it—like man."

Joseph fell quiet, knowing he was out of excuses.

"I'll respect you more for it."

Joseph finally looked at me, his brown eyes showing his weakness. "I'll double the amount I owe you. Eight million. Just let me go."

"Now we're talking." I adjusted the sleeve of my suit, meticulous about my appearance, like always. I wore power like a fresh suit, filling out the clothing as if it were made for me. An invisible crown sat upon my head, something I balanced at all times.

"I can get it to you in twenty-four hours," he said. "All in cash. Just let us go."

"A tempting offer." Now that we'd cut to the chase, things were a lot more interesting.

"Do we have a deal?" He adjusted his arms to get comfortable. The bite of the metal around his wrists must have been painful.

I gazed at his two cronies, both equally unimpressive. While they were burly with muscle, they didn't have true strength and agility. Their eyes hinted at stupidity, following orders without understanding what they were doing. That's how they got into this mess in the first place —because their boss was even dumber. "Money doesn't mean anything to me, Joseph. Reputation is everything."

His eyes fell with devastation. "I'll make it twelve

million."

The corner of my mouth rose in a smile. "You need to learn how to listen."

His rate of breathing increased, his chest rising and falling with his impending doom.

"I have an image to maintain. If I let you off the hook that easily, my other business partners won't hesitate to cross me. Obviously, I can't allow this."

"Don't kill me…" His voice shook in desperation. "I made a mistake. You've made mistakes too."

"But it wasn't a mistake." Now my voice deepened, my anger slowly growing to enormous proportions. "You aren't a child, Joseph. You understood what you were doing when you did it. Your only mistake was the idiotic belief that you could get away with it."

He bowed his head, his chest moving at a quicker pace.

"I don't accept your money. However, I'm going to let you go."

Joseph raised his head slowly, his eyes meeting mine with incredulity.

I had the perfect compensation for what he had done,

something you couldn't put a price on. I had no remorse for what I had done. It was my responsibility to make an example of my enemies—and I did it well. "I've stolen something from you worth more than money. I've taken something innocent—something pure. And you'll never get it back."

Now Joseph began to shake for entirely different reasons.

"I've taken your lovely sister, London. Now she's mine." I tilted my head and watched his expression, knowing his reaction would be utterly priceless. "She's on her way here now—to become my prisoner."

Joseph's jaw clenched before his eyes widened to the size of baseballs. He burst out of his seat like an angry bronco coming out of the chute. His forehead bulged with a thick vein and his face reddened to the color of a beet. "You motherfucker—"

Dunbar slugged him in the gut and slammed him back down into the chair. He punched him in the mouth for the insult he'd just unleashed my way. "Watch what you say to Mr. Donoghue. Might be your last words." He stood behind Joseph ominously, his arms crossed over his chest.

Joseph clenched his jaw again, frustrated. He was completely helpless to do anything, and that made his rage burn more brightly. His only family member in the world had been taken from him, and he had to sit there and play nice.

I almost felt bad for him—almost. "Would you rather me kill you?"

For an instant, his anger vanished as he considered the question. "Absolutely."

I cocked my head to the side, intrigued by the selfless response. Men like us used others as bulletproof vests, allowing a pile of victims to form around us so we remained untouched. But Joseph didn't hesitate before he gave me his answer. "Then I made the right decision."

The vein in his forehead bulged once more. His arms shook as he tried to break the chain of his handcuffs with only his strength. "She has nothing to do with this. Please, leave her alone."

When I got the detailed report about London, I was impressed. At a young age, she was already a medical student at NYU. At the top of her class, she was expected to go far. The guys told me she was a looker, with deep brown hair and hazel eyes. So, she had brains and beauty. It really was a shame she would live out the rest of her life in chains. "You should have thought this through before you crossed me, Joseph." I adjusted my watch on my wrist, feeling the smooth platinum with my fingertips.

"Cut off my hand, alright?" Spit flew from his mouth because he was talking so fast. "Just spare her."

"Sorry. I have to make an example of the people who cross me. Every time they see London chained to the wall during a business meeting, they'll think twice. When they witness her cruel treatment, her rags for clothes, they'll know deception isn't worth it."

Joseph yanked on the chains again. "This isn't right."

"No, it's not," I said simply. Most things in life weren't right. And it certainly wasn't fair. Like everyone else, I'd suffered once upon a time. But I changed my future rather than accepting it. Everyone had the choice—whether they realized it or not. "I will take her when I wish. My men will take her if they so choose. Every night, when you're sleeping in your warm bed, just know London is wishing for death."

His face turned pale as the blood drained from it. Instead of being livid, he looked terrified. Knowing his sister was facing a lifetime of cruel punishment because of his mishap must have been the heaviest form of guilt a man could experience.

"I'm gonna let you go, Joseph," I continued. "Your punishment will be to live. To live and know your sister's life was taken because of your stupidity. If you try to save her, I'll kill you. It's as simple as that." I snapped my fingers, cuing Dunbar into action.

Dunbar unlocked their handcuffs, letting their arms go free. Joseph massaged his wrists, which were red and sliced in some places. He stared me down with the same rage as before, but now it was mixed with grief.

I waited for him to do something, to make an attempt on my life. I hoped he would. Then I would get to snuff the life out of this man and still abuse his sister. It was a win-win. Everyone in my world would know I exercised complete power. I saw everything—even if I pretended not to.

Joseph finally stood up, his cronies following suit. Dunbar and the rest of my men escorted them outside while I remained in my chair. I didn't see him off, and once he was behind me, I didn't look back. My back was vulnerable and completely exposed, yet I didn't have a single care in the world.

Because whatever attack he made would miss the mark.

2

CREWE

The plane was already in the air before I began my conversation with Joseph. After they landed at the airport, they took my private helicopter and flew to the Shetland Islands, the northern tip of Scotland where I kept my residence. Subarctic, it was cold year round—but absolutely beautiful. I'd lived in many places during my lifetime, but the remote archipelago had a quaint quality I couldn't find anywhere else.

With a small population, Scandinavian influences were prevalent among the islands. Life moved at a slower pace, concentrating on old Scottish ways of life. Most inhabitants were Shetland breeders, the small horses that weren't much bigger than a pony. The grass was always green, and the ocean brought fresh air across the land on a daily basis. Full of wildlife, it was far removed from the bustling city and the rest of the United Kingdom.

My home had been built hundreds of years ago. I had to refurbish the interior, adding hardwood floors, central heating, and all the renovations that accommodated my eccentric taste. However, it still took on the appearance of a castle in the Scottish Highlands. It felt like a castle rather than a home, sometimes.

I sat in the living room, drinking my scotch and looking over a report from my distilleries where they created whiskey, making sure the blending was just right and still true to the flavor my ancestors created in the fifteenth century.

Ariel walked into the room in jeans with heels and a thick black sweater. Her brown hair was pulled back into an elegant updo. While she was soft on the eyes, she was hard on the inside. She was ruthless, authoritative, and cold—the best business partner I could ask for. "The helicopter is landing, Crewe."

I set my work on the coffee table, abandoning the smooth scotch that flowed down my throat with just the right amount of heat. "Thank you, Ariel." I buttoned the front of my suit then adjusted my watch. "We should give our new guest a proper greeting, shall we?" The corner of my mouth rose in a smile, knowing Joseph would pay for his recklessness until the day he died.

We left through the backdoor and crossed the short hawkweed and chickweed grass as we approached the helicopter that was slowly descending on the flat field. The property was right at the coastline and very secluded. I was never concerned neighbors would discover my criminal activities due to their proximity. The only way back to the Scottish mainland was by boat or helicopter. The help was in charge of gathering supplies we needed on a daily basis.

Ariel walked beside me as we approached the chopper. It landed on the grass with grace before the engine was shut off. The propeller still spun as the engine cooled down. We stood side by side as we waited for our guest.

Ariel's loose strands flew back in the wind from the propellers, and slowly, they fluttered until her hair was perfect once more. She placed her hands in her pockets, looking just as terrifying as me.

Dunbar came from the rear and joined us, his arm crossed over his muscular chest.

Ethan emerged from the helicopter carrying a woman in

his arms. She was unconscious, her head dangling over the edge of his arm. Her long brown hair blew in the wind. She wore dark jeans and a simple top, obviously used to the humid weather of New York City in the summertime.

She was in for a surprise.

Ethan carried her toward me, the rest of the team in tow. In a black hoodie and dark jeans, he carried London effortlessly. "She was a bit ornery. Had to put her under." He shifted her in his arms before he handed her off to Dunbar.

I took a peek at her, seeing the fair skin of her flawless cheeks. She had a small nose, full lips, and eyelashes that would make her eyes stand out if they were open. Petite in size, she didn't seem like she could put up much of a fight. "She reminds me of a puppy—so innocent."

Ethan chuckled. "This woman is not innocent. She almost got a hold of my gun. There's no doubt in my mind she would have pulled the trigger."

Now my interest was truly piqued. "Maybe she has more in common with Joseph than we realized." I nodded back toward the house. "Let's go."

We walked back inside and went downstairs to the basement. It was still in the formation of a prison, with cement flooring and walls. There was a small cot in the corner, a toilet and a sink, but nothing else. There weren't any windows because the basement extended deep into the ground. Only a few lights were on at a time, keeping my prisoner in near darkness.

Dunbar set her on the cot and pulled the blanket over her shoulders since she was frozen from the trek across the lawn. He pulled her hair out of her face and took a good look at her. "I'm excited for a go. She really is as beautiful as Ethan said." He left her on the cot then closed the door, locking her up in a cell made of steel bars. She had no privacy from anyone within the basement. But now that she was no longer a real person, it didn't matter. She was my retribution for what Joseph had done to me. I would get the four million dollars that was owed to me.

Actually, London would.

Everyone except my butler left for the day. Ariel and Dunbar took the helicopter back to the mainland, where they lived their own lives and spent their free time. I remained in the living room, drinking scotch in front of the fire and placing the cool glass against my temple when I felt a migraine coming on.

I enjoyed the peace and quiet this island provided. Sometimes it felt like just me and the sea, the waves crashing down against the cliff right outside my front window. I liked to keep the windows open so I could listen to the rhythmic sound. Something about its consistency stilled my nerves. Just like the sun would rise and set every single day, the waves would meet the shore, unaffected by any living man. The absolute power the elements had over mankind was fascinating to me.

I would be lying if I said I didn't crave that kind of power myself.

Thump.

I stopped breathing when I heard the sound.

Thump. Thump.

I concentrated on the sound to pinpoint where it was coming from. Sometimes the wind howled on a cruel night, but there hadn't been a storm in the forecast. I abandoned my scotch on the table and rose to my feet, thinking of where my weapons were stowed in the house, easily accessible from every room.

Thump.

My eyes darted to the ground, realizing exactly where the noise was coming from.

The basement.

My guest was awake.

I walked down the stairs to the basement wearing jeans and a t-shirt now that everyone had left for the day. After I opened the door, I peeked down the stairway and spotted London. She stood back on one leg and kicked the bars as hard as she could, trying to make them crack under her power. The force was so minimal, the bars didn't even shake. She aimed for the hinges of the door but that didn't make a difference either. Absorbed in her poor attempt to free herself, she didn't notice my light footsteps as I approached the bottom of the basement. "The only thing you're going to break is your knee."

At the sound of my voice, she stood back, her forehead gleaming with sweat and her hair messy from exerting herself. Her hands were still held in front of her body, prepared for anything.

I walked to the door and looked at her, noting the way her jeans hugged her curvy hips and thin legs. The gray V-neck she wore pointed to her tiny waist, her natural hourglass figure obvious. She was definitely pretty, but she didn't do anything for me. The guys talked about her like she was a perfect ten.

She was a perfect nobody to me.

"These bars are made out of steel, in case you didn't notice. And we're in the middle of the ocean on an island, so if you break something, you're on your own. All I've got is Tylenol." I stood at the bars and examined her, my arms crossed over my chest.

Despite her dire circumstance, she didn't seem scared. She only appeared calculating, her brain working furiously to figure out what her next move should be. She tried to find a solution rather than give in to the panic.

"It's time to make introductions. I'm Crewe—and I own you."

As if I had slapped her, her eyes narrowed into a threatening expression. "What did you just say to me?" She walked toward the bars, having no reluctance for coming close to me. If I slid my arm through the bars, I could grab her by the neck. "I don't give a damn who you are. You don't own me. Nobody owns me." She jabbed her finger into her chest, amplifying her meaning.

I liked her fire. She had a lot more courage than that pussy-shit brother of hers. "You'll change your mind…in time." I came closer to the bars, getting a better look at her. She had a nice mouth, wide with soft lips. I had the urge to run my thumb along her bottom lip, but I had no interest in kissing her. I just wanted to touch her—to pet her.

"I'm gonna get out of here. And when I do, I'm going to rip your eyes out of your head and shove them up your ass."

The threat was so unexpected I actually laughed. "Whoa, you've got quite the mouth on you." I chuckled from deep inside my chest. "But I like a woman with a dirty mouth."

She didn't let the implication deter her hatred. "Trust me, you aren't going to like me."

She was stuck in a prison with nowhere to run, but yet, she wouldn't drop her guard. She wouldn't drop her hostility or her pride. She could easily fall to her knees and weep. But she still stood on her own two feet—strong. "I think I already do."

Stupidly, she thought I wasn't paying attention to every single move she made. She waited until my eyes were locked on hers before she launched her hand through the opening between the bars and tried to grab my neck.

I'd been expecting it, so I dodged to the left and grabbed her wrist. I pinned her arm down, bending it at just the right angle to twist her elbow in an agonizing way. With just a little more pressure, I could've snapped it right in half.

She breathed through the pain but didn't wince. The fire was still in her eyes, refusing to let me believe I had any power over her.

Somehow, my respect grew. "Don't fuck with me, London." I pressed my lips against her ear, listening to her heavy breathing. "I promise, you'll lose." I released her arm, allowing her to keep it for another day.

She immediately pulled her arm back into the cage and stood where I couldn't reach her again.

"Smart girl."

She let her arm hang limply by her side, refusing to caress it despite the pain she must have been experiencing.

"The sooner you behave yourself, the better your life will be. We're on an island in the middle of the sea. There's nowhere for you to run or hide—unless you want to jump to your death from a cliff."

She stared at me with vicious eyes. "Doesn't sound so bad right now."

The corner of my mouth rose in a smile. "If you get your act together, you can visit the rest of the house. But if you'd rather put up this fight, then you can stay in here."

"I'm never going to act like an obedient dog, so it looks like I'm gonna stay down here." She moved to the cot and leaned against the wall, pulling her knees to her chest while she stared me down with pure hatred.

"It's awfully cold down here," I warned.

"Better than being any closer to you."

When I first saw her being carried off the helicopter, I had a completely different assumption about the kind of woman she was. I'd assumed she would be like everyone else, whiny and weak. I assumed her backbone would be just as soft as her cheek. But she took someone like me by surprise—which was difficult. "In case you haven't noticed, there's not a shower down here."

Her expression didn't change.

"You won't be allowed to take one until you behave yourself."

"People used to only bathe once a year," she countered. "I'll be fine."

I chuckled, loving the fact she had a response to everything I said. "Give it a week, and see if you change your mind."

She pulled the thin blanket over her legs to keep warm. "If you're done taunting me, you can leave."

She was excusing me? "You don't have any questions?"

"No."

"You don't want to know why you're here?"

"It's obvious."

It was? "How so?"

"I don't live under a rock," she said coldly. "I know I've been abducted into sex trafficking. But I'm not worried about it because there's a solution to every problem. I will find one."

The smile left my face. "This isn't school, London.

There's not a solution to every problem. Life isn't as simple as a mathematical equation. I'm one of the greatest criminals of the underworld. I'm the kind of problem with no solution. I'm the kind of problem that can't be solved. The situation you're in is far worse than being sold into slavery—because you're my slave."

3

CREWE

I walked into Ariel's office. "What's on the agenda?"

She remained at her desk, her black glasses sitting on the bridge of her nose. She spun a pen in her fingertips as she pressed her lips tightly together. "We have a new buyer in Ireland. Wants to buy a large order of Highland Whiskey. And when I say large, I mean enormous."

"How enormous are we talking?" I fell into the chair and unbuttoned the front of my black suit.

"We'd need to hire an extra crew just to oversee the production. You were thinking of expanding anyway. Perhaps we should pursue that now."

If a business wasn't growing, then it was at risk. That's how I saw it. "Let's do it."

She made some notes. "Alright. I'll take care of it."

"Anything else?"

"Yes. Her Highness Wilhelmina is having a ball next weekend. Of course, you're on the invite list."

"Excellent." I rested my fingertips against my lips as I listened to her. "What else?"

"We haven't heard anything from—"

"Sir, I'm sorry to interrupt." Finley walked inside, wearing slacks and a collared shirt. "London refuses everything I make for her. It's been three days, so I thought I would bring it to your attention."

I tried not to smile at the information. "I'll take care of it, Finley. Thank you."

"She hasn't been drinking anything either." He gave a slight bow before he walked out, closing the door behind him.

Ariel pulled the glasses off the bridge of her nose and rested them on the desk. She was just a few years younger than me, but her reading glasses aged her at least ten years. "Our guest has been a bit of a fuss, from what I understand."

"She's interesting…" There was no better way to put it. "Has a bigger backbone than Joseph."

"So do a lot of people," she jabbed.

I chuckled then rose to my feet, buttoning the front of my suit again. "I'll get her under control soon enough. That's when the real fun will begin."

Ariel smiled before I walked out. "We'll finish this conversation when you're ready, sir."

I walked across the house until I reached the entrance to the basement. The house was two stories tall, and it seemed like a mile from one end of the house to the other. I descended the staircase and found her sitting on the cot, stacks of food piled up on the opposite side of the cell.

When she realized I'd come for a visit, she turned her head in my direction, keeping her eyes glued to my movements.

"No appetite?"

"Maybe your servant just isn't a good cook."

She was the biggest smartass I had ever met. "I could make you something. And I'm definitely a good cook."

"No, thanks. I'll pass on the poison."

I rested my elbows on the bars as I examined her in the cell. A quiet chuckle escaped my throat, quiet enough for only me to hear. "What's your plan, London? Starve yourself to death?"

"Starve myself until I figure out a way to get out of here."

"You expect to overpower me after fasting for three days?" I asked incredulously. Even if she were healthy, she would stand no chance against me.

Her silence told me she didn't have a comeback —for once.

"Eat."

"I'm not stupid. I'm sure you slipped something into my food to knock me out."

"And why would I do that?"

She looked away. "Let's not beat around the bush."

I understood her implication. "Lovely, if I wanted to fuck you, I would hold you down and do it. I wouldn't knock you out first. It's not nearly as much fun that way."

Her face immediately drained of all color.

"Now shut up and eat."

She still didn't move for the food, probably wanting to wait until I was out of the room.

"So, do you have any questions?" She still didn't know why she was here, on the other side of the world and away from the life she once knew. I wanted her to know that her brother was responsible for her demise, that if she blamed anyone, it should be him.

"Nope."

Her stubbornness baffled me. It was worse than mine. "I guess you don't want that shower then?"

"I'll pass." She looked to the left side of the room, ignoring me like I wasn't even there.

I didn't expect it to take this long to get her to cooperate. I expected her to be somewhat scared after the initial shock wore off. But this woman was too courageous, too proud to give in to the fear.

So I'd have to make her give in to the fear.

Swiftly and silently, I unlocked the door and crept into her cell. The lights were off, and she lay in the small cot, the air freezing. I leaned over her, prepared to grab her by the neck.

But she must have heard me because she struck first. She threw her hand upward, aiming right for my eyes.

I was annoyed that she was so in tune with her surroundings. She didn't trust her environment, not even for a second. For a woman in medical school, she had the reflexes of an assassin.

But I easily overpowered her, pinning her hand down along with the rest of her body. I forced my weight on top of her, keeping her against the hard cot and immobilizing her. I stared her down and watched her twist and turn underneath me, doing whatever she could to get free.

But nothing worked.

She eventually gave up her struggle when I didn't move an inch. Like a mountain, she couldn't move me with only sheer determination. Her hands finally went limp, and she stared at me with defeat in her eyes, not fear. "Let go of me."

My voice came out as a whisper. "Make me."

Fire glowed in her eyes, and she tried to throw me off with her hips.

But it was pointless.

She tried pushing me off her body with her legs, but that didn't work either. She hissed between her teeth, sweaty and out of breath from the pointless exertion. She was too small and weak to overpower someone like me.

However, I did enjoy watching the fight. "You can't beat me. Stop trying."

"I'll never stop trying," she said through her heavy breathing. "One day, your guard is going to be down, and I'm going to hit you where it hurts."

I separated her thighs with my knees, positioning her underneath me with a hint of sexual violence.

She stiffened, the terror finally entering her face. It was the first time she showed an ounce of fear. It was a trigger I suspected I could hit. I would use her body to make her feel dirty, defiled. "Don't…" It was the first plea, the first beg.

The ball was back in my court, and I felt a surge of adrenaline. I pressed my face closer to hers, feeling her breath fall on my lips. "You don't want me to fuck you? I promise, you'll like it."

She stared into my eyes, all her courage and strength completely gone.

I had the upper hand, the power. And I would use that to my full advantage. "If you don't want me to, say please."

Her lips parted, but the word didn't escape. Her hesitance stemmed from stubbornness, not true desire. She didn't like giving in to me, following any kind of command. She knew that would give me the small amount of power she possessed.

My hand moved to the top of my jeans, and I undid the button.

"Please." She spit out the word quickly, squirming underneath me.

"Please, what?"

"Please don't do it…" She couldn't say the R word, the terrifying word every woman never wanted to say.

I exerted my dominance, my control—and that was all I wanted. I got off her and stood on my feet. "You're coming with me. Now."

"Where?" She immediately crawled into the corner of the cot like a frightened animal. She pulled her knees to her chest, trying to hide behind them.

I stood over the cot, piercing her with my terrifying gaze. "Get your ass up now." I grabbed her by the ankle and yanked her off the bed until her back hit the floor. Then I grabbed her by the hair and pulled her to her feet. "Do as I say or I'll make you do as I say." I yanked her head back so her eyes were focused on the ceiling, my lips pressed to her ear. "Any questions?"

"No."

I released the knot of hair and walked out of the cell.

She caught her breath then followed me, her eyes on me the entire time.

I shut the door behind her then pointed to the stairs. "Up."

She walked up first, moving until she reached the door. It was unlocked, so she stepped inside.

My hand moved to the back of her neck, but I didn't dig my fingers into the skin the way I would have liked. I guided her to the other side of the house, moving past the grand dining room, the vaulted ceilings of the entryway, and the first living room with a large hearth that still burned with firewood.

I took her to the second floor and into the bedroom she would soon be occupying. The large bathroom had a spacious shower, one with a glass door that opened and closed. I guided her inside then released her once she was in front of the shower. "Take off your clothes." She'd been wearing them for four days now. They were about to go into the trash—to be forgotten.

The feistiness returned to her eyes. She stared at me in offense, unable to believe the command I just gave her.

"Did you not hear me?" I asked through clenched teeth, not wanting to waste time with another argument.

"I'll take off my clothes if you shut the door."

I shook my head. "That's not how it works, lovely."

"Don't call me that," she hissed.

"What do you prefer? Slave?"

She raised her hand and tried to slap me across the face.

I almost let her, but since establishing authority was more important right now, I snatched her by the wrist and yanked her arm to her side. Then I backhanded her across the cheek, slapping her hard enough to make the skin redden.

She sucked in a short breath at the hit. Her head remained turned the other way, in shock that I actually did it.

I grabbed her by both shoulders and shook her. "If you don't want me to slap you, don't slap me. If you don't want me to hurt you, do as I say. If you don't want me to fuck you on that bed in the other room, take off your clothes and get your ass in the shower." I squeezed her hard before I finally let her go.

I leaned against the wall and crossed my arms over my chest, waiting for her to do as I commanded.

She pulled her hair out of her face, her cheek turning red where my palm collided with the skin. Tears weren't in her eyes, but she finally looked defeated, understanding that obeying my commands was better than defying me.

She felt the bottom of her shirt but didn't pull it over her head. She tried to think of a way out of her situation, but unfortunately, there was nothing she could do. She had to pay the price of her brother's stupidity—even if it wasn't fair.

She finally pulled her top over her head, revealing a white bra underneath. Her tits formed a cleavage line down the middle, and it was the first time my cock thickened in interest. I had a long line of women in my life, and I never mixed business with pleasure, but seeing the natural swell of a rack was a bit of a turn on.

She opened the shower door and turned on the warm water, letting it get hot as she unbuttoned her jeans and pulled them down her long legs. She didn't make eye contact as she stripped down to her underwear, full of shame that she was giving in to my demands.

She hesitated when she was left in only underwear, knowing I was going to see every inch of her bare skin in just a moment.

I watched her in her black panties, still aroused even though she wasn't wearing a thong. She had long and slender legs, the kind that would look kissable in heels. Her stomach was lined with muscles, subtle and sexy. Her arms were slender but defined by the grooves of muscle. She must have hit the gym a few times a week, probably to blow off steam after studying around the clock.

She undid her bra and let it come loose. But before she took it off, she turned around so I couldn't see her tits head-on.

I almost commanded her to turn around.

She set the bra on top of her pile of clothes then reached for her panties. Now she just wanted to get it over with, because she bent over and yanked them off before she stepped into the shower. But she didn't move quick enough to stop me from seeing the pink skin of her pussy and a glimpse of her small asshole.

Now I really was hard.

She got into the shower and shut the door behind her, the warm water greeting her. Her hair clung to her neck once it was wet, and she grabbed a bottle of shampoo and massaged her scalp, ridding it of the oil and grime.

I watched the water roll down her luscious body, peering through the steam that pressed against the glass doors. My cock twitched in my jeans the longer I stared at her. My arousal coursed through me at a blinding speed. I would have to make a trip to Glasgow to see one of my regulars. My cock needed to be sucked soon.

She stayed under the water for a long time, much longer than necessary. She probably cherished the feeling of cleanliness. Up until that point, she'd been stuck in the same clothes as the oil built up on her scalp and skin. Now that she had to go without this luxury, she truly appreciated it.

"That's long enough," I commanded.

She stared at the faucet before she turned it off, ending her shower.

I grabbed a thick towel and handed it to her, feeling my cock press against the fly of my jeans.

She immediately covered herself with it, hiding her nakedness even though I'd already seen all the good stuff. She patted herself dry, finally looking at me again with the same displeasure.

"You should dry your hair. Might get sick." I pointed to the hair dryer.

She eyed the hair dryer before she looked at me again. "Like I care about getting sick."

"Well, I do. I don't want you to give it to me." I smiled, trying to make a joke to wipe off the sour look on her face.

She just looked angrier.

She dried her hair quickly, using her fingers to comb through the strands as she kept the towel around her chest. When she was finished, she moved to grab her clothes, which were now gone. "What did you do with them?"

"You aren't wearing those anymore." I picked up the outfit sitting on the bed. "This is what you're wearing now." It was a long gray dress with sleeves, made from thick cotton. It was the perfect size for her narrow waist, highlighting her curvy features around her chest, stomach, and ass.

She tightened the towel around her torso as she stared at the dress in disappointment. "I'm supposed to wear that in the cell?"

"You could wear it up here—if you behaved yourself."

She snatched the dress and headed back to the bathroom.

"I don't think so, lovely. You can get dressed in front of me." I sat at the foot of the bed and leaned back on my elbows.

The look she gave me was full of even more hatred than ever before. She pulled on the panties underneath her towel and managed to get the bra on in the same way. Then she abandoned the towel altogether and pulled the dress over her head. Even without makeup or styling her hair, she pulled it off.

She still had an attitude, but at least she was obeying me. "What we do next is your call." I was tempted to command her to ride my cock, but I didn't think she would actually do it. She was scared of me, but not scared enough.

"How so?"

"Personally, I don't want to keep you in a cell like a rat. It's awfully cold and dark down there."

She crossed her arms over her chest.

"But if you keep acting up, you won't leave me much choice."

She looked out the bedroom window but couldn't see anything since it was pitch black outside. It was two in the morning, so dawn was hours away. "What do you want from me? If you aren't putting me into sex trafficking."

She'd finally started to ask questions. "It's pretty simple. Your brother tried to rip me off during a business deal. He tried to steal four million dollars from me. With the business I run, that kind of betrayal can't slide. So, I took something valuable from him—you."

Her arms slowly moved to her sides, and she forgot about her situation—for a heartbeat. "What kind of business do you run?"

"I sell intelligence. And he bought it."

"Intelligence for what?" she asked. "My brother is a retirement advisor. He travels the world and tries to get people to invest in IRAs and SEPs."

The only reason why I didn't laugh was because I actually pitied her. "Sorry, lovely. He lied to you."

She lowered her gaze, her eyes shifting back and forth as her mind worked quickly.

"When I told him you were the price he was going to pay, he wasn't happy. But that's how it goes."

She came back to the conversation. "And what are you going to do with me?"

"That remains to be seen. But I can assure you, it'll be in whatever way I can cause him the most pain." I left the bed and stood, towering over her with my height. "It's nothing personal, London. You're just a victim in this game we're playing."

The hatred was gone from her expression. Now she continued to think quietly to herself, trying to understand the madness she had been thrown into. She was a prisoner in a foreign land, having no rights whatsoever. Whatever fear she had was hidden deep below the surface. "It is personal," she whispered. "When you take my life away, it's very personal."

4

LONDON

I asked to be returned to the basement because it was the only environment I knew. But the longer I sat in the dark, even with new clothes and clean hair, the more the paranoia began to sink in. I'd put on a brave face for as long as I could, but my strength was fading away. The man keeping me here wasn't like any other man I had ever met.

He was strong.

Smart.

Powerful.

When he laid his body on top of mine, that's when the truth sank into my bones. He was an opponent I couldn't defeat. I couldn't use my size or my intelligence against him. When I was cornered like a rat, there was nowhere for me to hide.

It would be so easy for me to freak out right now.

But I'm not gonna break down.

I'm gonna stay calm and try to figure this out.

Crewe threatened to rape me, but he didn't. He saw me naked, but he still didn't force himself on me. He was difficult to read, but even though he granted me some mercy, I knew he was extremely dangerous.

He had a whole team kidnap me and transfer me to this freezing island. I knew we were somewhere up north, somewhere out of the country. It was so different than the swelling humidity of New York City. I missed the sun and heat so much—like never before.

My cot was uncomfortable, but the food was tolerable. I suspected if I ate it when it was fresh, it would actually be pretty good. I had a private toilet, so at least I didn't have to use it in front of anyone. Crewe allowed me to keep some dignity.

The news about Joseph was terrifying. If he had any connection to a man like Crewe, I had to believe he wasn't really a retirement salesman. He truly was mixed up with bad people, serious criminals like the man who currently had me trapped.

But one thing kept me calm.

Joseph knew Crewe had captured me.

Maybe I didn't know my brother as well as I thought I did. But I knew he loved me fiercely, and he would do anything to protect me. There wasn't a doubt in my mind that he was working on a plan to get me out of here.

I just had to be patient.

Staying in this basement would make things more difficult. I had to get to the surface, to check out the rest of the house. If Joseph made his move, having me down here would just make my rescue more difficult.

So I would have to do something I strongly didn't want to do.

I would have to obey Crewe.

———

Crewe brought me breakfast the following morning instead of sending his butler, Finley. Dressed in a midnight black suit, his broad shoulders looked utterly masculine. Without being able to see his skin, it was obvious he was packed with lean muscle. He had dark brown hair that nearly looked black, a five o'clock shadow on his chin even though he probably just shaved a few hours ago, and he had an arrogant smile on those full lips. He slid the tray of food under the bars then stood to his full height, something over six feet.

When I saw my captor for the first time, I was surprised by his appearance. I expected a monster, a disgusting middle aged man who had nothing better to do than kidnap young women. I expected him to be fat and flabby, a fiend who couldn't get women on his own.

But Crewe could definitely get women on his own.

If I saw him on my morning walk to the coffee shop in Manhattan, I'd probably stop just to strike up a conversation with him, hoping it would lead to a date for the weekend. I didn't have a problem being forward with men. Time was important to me, and I liked to get to the point as quickly as possible. If he wasn't into me, that was just fine. I would find someone who was.

Crewe stood at the door of my cell, his hands sliding into the pockets of his slacks. "Morning."

I bit my tongue just so I wouldn't say anything. Something about his air of arrogance just made me want to defy him. It had nothing to do with the fact that he had kidnapped me from my bed and taken me to the other side of the world. Something about him immediately put me on edge and made me want to ignore his requests just to annoy him. He was the kind of man who got under my skin—but I had no idea why.

He stared at me with his handsome face, his chiseled features and pretty brown eyes. They were mocha, warm and radiant. They matched everything about him perfectly, hinting at a dark core. "Didn't sleep well, lovely?"

I knew he called me that just to annoy me. "My day was going pretty well until you showed up."

He chuckled, his eyes lighting up at the same time. "I thought I was being a nice guy by bringing you breakfast. Should I have brought flowers instead?"

"You should have brought cash and a passport."

He smiled, amused by my smartass comments. "You're smart. I guess it makes sense since you're a doctor."

"I'm not a doctor. I would be training to become one right now if you hadn't kidnapped me."

"How far along were you in school?"

I ignored the question, not wanting to chit-chat.

He slid his arms through the bars as he relaxed, probably daring me to try something. He wanted any opportunity to exert his power over me. He baited me into making attacks so he could squish me like a bug. "If you calm down, I'll invite you upstairs. It's a beautiful house. It's been restored but the natural history of the castle has been preserved. You seem like someone who would appreciate it."

"Why is that?"

"Because you've been living in a rat hole for a week."

I nearly laughed at his wit.

"So, what's it gonna be? Are you gonna play nice?"

"What does that mean, exactly?" I sat on my cot and kept my knees together so he wouldn't see up my dress. "Because I'll never be pleasant company."

"That makes two of us. I just don't want you to attack Finley or Ariel. They're good people."

"Who's Ariel?"

He grinned like I said something particularly interesting. "Jealous, lovely?"

"No, idiot," I snapped. "I've met Finley. I haven't seen this Ariel person before."

"She's my business partner."

"Oh." My insides turned in anger. Another woman was in the house, knowing I was locked up down here. How could she stand aside and not give a damn? How could she call herself a woman and do nothing? I hadn't even met the woman, and I hated her. "Well, you don't have to worry about that. If I'm gonna make a move on anyone, it'll be you."

"Ooh…I hope it's the kind of move I like." He winked.

The fact that I thought he was charming—even for an instant—irritated me. This guy was a psychopath with a good sense of humor. That was it.

"I can settle for that." He unlocked the door and opened it. "Grab your breakfast and eat at the table upstairs."

I stared at the open door, unable to believe he was actually letting me out. "You're really so naïve to think I won't try to hurt you?"

He grinned like my words had no impact. "Lovely, I'd like to see you try."

"Stop calling me that."

"Would you prefer Slave?" he asked. "Because that has a nice ring to it too."

I couldn't handle a title like that, so I shut my mouth. Lovely was much better.

"Lovely it is." He nodded to the stairway. "After you."

I stopped myself from rolling my eyes and reached the next floor. With my plate still in hand, I walked to the table. My plate contained scrambled eggs, a slice of toast, and a piece of bacon. It wasn't much, but since I wasn't eating much anyway, it was perfect.

I didn't see much of the first floor last time I was released from my cage. I'd been too terrified of Crewe to think about anything besides him. I concentrated on how close he was to me, the way he moved his hands as he walked. In anticipation of a strike, I kept my eyes on him.

But now I knew I was safe—for the time being.

"This way." Crewe led the way into the enormous kitchen. It had two ovens, two microwaves, and enough kitchen space to prepare dinner for dozens of people. A kitchen table sat beside the large window that took up most of the wall. "Would you like some coffee?"

I set my plate down and immediately looked outside, wanting to get an idea of where I was. But I only saw rocks jutting out until they disappeared over a cliff, and the ocean sea in the background. Beyond that, it was only blue. Infinite blue. The sight was beautiful, but it made me realize just how alone I was.

There was no escape.

Crewe studied my face, watching my expression change. His brown eyes contrasted against everything around the property, from the green of the grass to the deep blue of the sea. "Don't make me ask you again."

The tone in his voice brought me back to reality. "Yes, please."

"So you do have manners." He walked to the counter and poured hot coffee into a mug. "I was beginning to think you didn't with all those smartass comments." He returned and placed the mug next to my plate. "Cream or sugar?"

"No, thank you." I growled when my automatic response came out, wanting to be as rude to him as possible.

He smiled. "I'll be in my office if you need me. Enjoy breakfast, and feel free to take a walk."

Was he serious? "You're just going to leave me alone? Outside?"

He stepped away with his hands in his pockets, his shirt tucked tightly around his waist. He had a wide chest, obviously powerful by the way he held himself. He had lean and long legs, the kind with muscled thighs that filled out his slacks well. "What are you going to do? Swim to Scotland?"

"We're in Scotland?" I blurted.

"No." He shifted his weight, his shoulders remaining straight no matter how he positioned his body. "We're in the Shetland islands—north of Scotland. About four hundred and fifty kilometers away. So, if you'd like to swim there, best of luck to you."

My jaw dropped inadvertently, the stress of the situation falling heavily on my shoulders. I was far away from home, across the Atlantic, on a remote island. No wonder why it was so freezing.

"We're on Fair Isle, the most remote island of the archipelago. My one and only neighbor lives on the other side of the island. It's a vacation home, so they only come to visit once a year."

"For the holidays?" If I knew when they were there, I could pound on their door and demand they call for help.

He gave me a cold stare, knowing exactly what I was trying to do.

Now I felt like an idiot for thinking he was an idiot.

"There are no landlines here. We only use satellite phones. There's Wi-Fi, but all the electronics are synced to my thumbprint. So don't bother."

"Wow…you've obviously kidnapped people before."

He didn't smile at the comment. "Enjoy your day." He walked around me, his masculine scent washing over me as he passed. "And if you hurt Finley or Ariel, I'll do the same to you. Finley is an innocent old man who is simply looking for peace. And Ariel isn't a woman much different from you. Don't. Touch. Them."

"But you have no problem with me trying to kill you?" For a man so cold, it was odd that he had affection for two people he wasn't related to.

"Do your worst, Lovely. I'll enjoy punishing you for it."

I stood on the cliff with my arms wrapped tightly around my stomach. The wind was mild, but the closer I got to the edge, the more the wind picked up. My hair flew behind my shoulders, and my arms prickled with goose bumps.

I noticed Finley leave the house and approach me, but I tried to ignore him, wanting to be left alone. Being so isolated from the rest of civilization was utterly terrifying. I was stuck with a madman who was using me to get revenge on my brother. I didn't have a clue what he would do to me—or how evil he really was.

Joseph, you better be looking for me.

If he didn't come for me, I wouldn't know what to do. Even if I killed everyone, how would I get off this island? Crewe had a helicopter, but I couldn't fly one if I tried—no matter how smart I was. There wasn't a boat, as far as I could tell. But Ariel must leave every day. Unless she lived there. Was she really his business partner? Maybe she was his wife. He didn't seem like the husband type.

"Lady London?" Finley was an older man, his Scottish accent heavy. He had brown hair tinted with red and a few freckles on his face. He had to be in his late sixties despite how easy it was for him to get around.

I realized in that moment Crewe didn't have a Scottish accent. It was American—just like mine.

Interesting.

"Yes?" I turned to him, feeling my heart soften when I saw the thick jacket and pair of binoculars he held.

"Mr. Donoghue was worried you might get cold out here." He wrapped the jacket around my shoulders. Since it was three sizes too big and Finley was a petite man, I assumed it belonged to Crewe himself. "And he wanted you to have these." He handed over the binoculars. "If you look along the rocks, you can see seals and penguins. There's wildlife everywhere."

"Oh…" I held the heavy binoculars in my hands and nodded. "Thank you."

He nodded then headed back to the house.

It didn't matter how cute and charming Finley was. I couldn't let that sweet old man get to me just because he gave me a jacket and a pair of binoculars. My goal was to get off this island and back to my life. I belonged in the hot and humid city of New York. I should be doing my rounds at the hospital this very moment. Even if I made my way back there, I would still be missing lectures and rotations. Hopefully, the university would grant me some leeway because of the extreme circumstances.

I spent the next few hours walking around the island, appreciating the beautiful flowers and the unique grass. Despite the circumstances, I couldn't deny how beautiful this was place. It was rich in botanical life.

I found a good spot along the cliff and watched seals swim around looking for fish. Some of them crawled up onto the rocks to enjoy the sunlight, their rubbery skin heating up despite the cold wind. The binoculars were helpful, and I found myself laughing when the seals fell asleep and accidentally rolled off the rocks and landed in the water.

"They're funny, aren't they?" Crewe was in his jeans and a long sleeved shirt. He sat beside me on the rock and looked down into the water.

The second he was next to me, I was on edge. My day had been peaceful until his presence ruined everything. I had to ignore some of the sweet things he did because he was evil underneath that pretty package. It didn't matter how ruggedly handsome he was. If I had the opportunity to kill him, I would take it. "They're fun to watch."

"The other islands have Shetland ponies—it's what the islands are known for."

"Why?"

"There are a lot of breeders here."

I placed the binoculars on the grass between us, just in case he wanted to use them.

"There's a bedroom for you upstairs if you'd like to sleep there."

I didn't want to go back to that cage underground. There was no sunlight, no fresh air. It was freezing cold, and that cot was no better than the cement. Even though I was outside in the cold, having his jacket around my body gave me the most warmth I'd felt since I arrived here. "I guess."

Crewe looked into the distance, staring at the deep blue ocean that stretched on forever.

"You don't have a Scottish accent." It wasn't a question, but I didn't know how to ask him anything. We were enemies, after all.

"I do." Fluidly, he switched into a Scottish accent, pronouncing each syllable with perfection as if he'd been born speaking that way. "I also have a British accent." He changed again, sounding like a lad from London.

"Why do you have an American accent?"

"Because you're American. Thought it might make you feel more comfortable."

"Since when do you care about making me more comfortable?" I snapped. "And why do you know all these different accents?"

He ignored my abrasive comments. "I work with a lot of different people in different places. Accents are important. They allow you to be accepted into different cultures more readily."

"What do you do when you aren't kidnapping people?" I asked, partially sarcastic.

"I have a lot of different trades. That's all you need to know."

"Good talk," I said bitterly.

He stood up and extended his hand to me. "Dinner is ready. I came to get you."

I stared at his hand then looked away, refusing to touch my enemy. Maybe he was nice now, but just the other night he threatened to rape me if I didn't strip down and shower in front of him. I got to my feet on my own and grabbed the binoculars.

Crewe didn't seem to care about my brush off. "Did you have a good day?" He walked beside me back to the house, his hands moving into his pockets.

"As good as it could be, I suppose."

We spent the rest of the walk in silence and entered the house. Finley had dinner on the table in the dining room, a separate room that could house fifty guests. The table was long, hinting of ancient royalty. I eyed the old wood before I sat down, feeling awkward for dining with my captor.

A few candles were lit, and our plates were set in front of us. Our dinner was freshly caught fish and greens.

I almost didn't eat it because I was disgusted that I had to eat with Crewe.

He ate quietly, not seeming to pay any attention to me.

"Is Ariel your wife?" I picked up my fork and finally took a bite.

"No." He didn't pull his gaze away from his food. "Why?"

"It just seems odd that she's just your business partner."

"Why?" He looked at me, his stare cold. "Because she's a woman? That's an awfully sexist comment coming from a woman aspiring to be a doctor."

"That's not how I meant it."

"Oh really? Didn't seem like it."

"I'm surprised because you seem like a sexist pig. After all, I'm being held here against my will." I gave him a look that conveyed just how much I hated him. "Let's not forget that. We aren't two friends having dinner together."

"I'm not as evil as you make me out to be." He sipped his scotch, an odd pairing with fish.

"I strongly disagree."

"Joseph stole four million dollars from me. For some idiotic reason, he thought he was going to get away with it. When he took a job dealing with criminal intelligence, he knew his loved ones would be targets if he crossed anyone. And from my research, it seems like you're his only living blood relative."

I held his gaze and didn't waver despite the emotion in my heart. My parents were killed by a drunk driver while they were out having a date night. A speeding car T-boned them into a tree, and they both died on impact. Joseph and I were just kids at the time.

"So he knew what he was risking, but he did it anyway. He's the evil one, not me. If I had a single person I loved, you can bet your ass I wouldn't mess around." He drank his scotch again, resting his elbow on the table. "I have a reputation to maintain. Joseph doubled the amount of money he owed, but that isn't enough after what he did. The only way to maintain my power was to do something terrifying—which is why I took you. I'm not evil, London. I'm just trying to survive—like everyone else."

"And how will anyone know you took me?" I questioned. "As far as I can tell, no one even knows we exist out here."

"They'll know." He swirled his glass before he took another drink. "Trust me on that."

My heart fell into the pit of my stomach. He had a plan for me. I wouldn't remain on Fair Isle forever. I didn't consider this place to be home, but I wasn't stupid. I knew there were far worse places out there. At least living here gave me the luxury of having some freedom. "What are you going to do to me?" I asked the question even though I knew I wasn't ready to hear the answer.

"It doesn't matter. You'll see soon enough."

I didn't touch my dinner because I lost my entire appetite. There wasn't a doubt in my mind that Crewe was a capable man. He had the power to do anything to me, and I would be powerless to stop him. If he wanted to rape me, he could. If he wanted to kill me, he could. If he wanted to do something far worse to me, I couldn't stop it.

Now I truly was terrified—of the unknown.

5

CREWE

Ariel knocked on my open office door. "You wanted to see me, Crewe?"

I paused my email to look at her. "Could you contact Bones and invite him over for dinner tomorrow night? Tell him I want to introduce him to someone."

She nodded. "Of course. I'll let you know what he says."

"Thank you."

Ariel walked out, leaving the office door open.

I turned back to my email, and a few minutes later, I received another guest.

"So, this is where all the magic happens?" In dark jeans and a designer blouse, London walked inside. Her hair was done today, shiny and long. Makeup was on her face, something Dunbar brought with him once he returned from Glasgow. When she put in the effort to look nice, she really shined. It surprised me that Joseph had a sister so much better looking than he was.

"Yes. A lot of magic." I turned in my seat to face her, my hands resting in my lap. My eyes roamed over her body without shame, knowing she was mine to do whatever I wanted with. I was the kind of man who appreciated a woman's curves—and I was appreciating hers. I'd seen her naked, and while the sight got me hard, she was malnourished and dirty. Now that she was regularly hygienic, she turned my head a few times. I wasn't entirely impressed with her because it took a lot for a woman to floor me, but I wasn't disappointed either.

She walked farther into the room and examined my desk.

"If you're looking for ways to kill me, be more discreet about it." When I slept in the same house as her, a part of me hoped she would make an attempt on my life. If she did, I would feel no guilt pinning her to my mattress and fucking her so hard she screamed. It would be a fair punishment for the crime—in my eyes.

"Actually, I wasn't—right now."

"Then why are you here?"

"Why do you think? I'm bored." She crossed her arms over her chest and shifted her weight to one leg. "I was in medical school, working sixteen hour days. And now I don't know what to do with myself."

I gave her a smoldering look, feeling my cock do all the thinking. "I can entertain you on this desk." I nodded to the dark wood where my computer and stationery sat. "Trust me, you wouldn't be bored again."

She rolled her eyes and walked to the window. "I'll pass."

I stared at her ass in her jeans, noting how tight it was. "You pretend not to be interested, but I think it's pretty obvious you are."

"Interested in what?" she asked incredulously.

"Me. If you hate me so much, why are you in here?"

She turned around and met my gaze. But she didn't have a response.

I rose out of my chair and stood behind my desk. "If you want me, all you have to do is ask." My hands moved to the wood below me, and my fingers felt the smooth polish. "I'm at your service anytime."

She made a look of disgust. "I knew you were arrogant, but wow."

"Wow what?" I asked.

"You just assume everyone wants to sleep with you?"

"Only kidnapped women who voluntarily spend time with me."

She knew she didn't have a logical counterargument to that. She pressed her lips tightly together as she stared me down, trying to think of something to say.

I knew she didn't have a goddamn excuse.

Ariel walked back into the room. "Bones said he'll be in the area, and he'd love to join you."

I never took my eyes off London. "Ariel, you've met our guest, haven't you?"

"No, I haven't." Ariel looked London up and down but didn't extend her hand. "Now I can put a face to the name."

"And I can put a face to evil," London snapped. "This

THE SCOTCH KING | 67

guy is holding me here against my will, and you don't care at all?"

Ariel stared at her coldly, the same look she gave me when she was pissed at me. "You expect me to care just because I'm a woman? I don't care about your problems. Whine to someone who gives a damn." She walked out, her head held high.

London shook her head like she couldn't believe what she just heard. "Everyone here is twisted."

"Maybe you're the one who's twisted. You don't belong in our world. Of course you don't understand it."

"But our worlds have the same laws. And kidnapping is illegal no matter what world you live in."

I smiled. "Not in mine."

Sooner or later, I knew she would make her move.

She would try to kill me, and since she knew she couldn't overpower me, she would try to do it while I was asleep. I purposely kept my door unlocked since I was a light sleeper. The second I heard her footsteps outside, I would be aware.

And then she came.

I heard the doorknob gently twist, the sound announcing her approach. I remained in bed and waited for her, my cock getting hard at the thought of what would happen next. She would try to choke me or slam something into my head. Instead, I would fuck her to teach her a lesson.

And I'd have every right to.

I felt her approach my bed slowly, her breathing steady. Despite her petite size, the floorboards still slightly creaked under her steps. The house was old, once a beautiful castle, but time had worn down several aspects of it.

Once she was close enough, I made my move. I grabbed her wrist and slammed it down on my nightstand, forcing the rock in her hand to come loose and topple to the ground. She screamed at the impact of her hand, either from the pain or the surprise.

I gripped the back of her neck and pulled her onto the bed, moving around her at the same time. I slept in the nude, so I was prepared for what would happen next. I yanked her bottoms and panties off until my cock was pressed right between her ass cheeks. I grinded against her, her hands pinned behind her back while my other hand held her by the neck. "I was hoping you would do that."

She breathed deeply underneath me, her body trying to fight me during her panic. "Don't—"

I pressed my tip to her entrance, sliding my head inside. I was greeted by her tightness, and I moaned automatically when I realized how much her pussy would squeeze my dick. "It's time to punish you."

"No." She bucked her hips back, but that didn't stop me.

"I'm gonna fuck you, London. And I'm gonna fuck you hard."

She bucked against me again and began to scream even though Finley wouldn't do a damn thing. "I'm sorry, okay? I'm sorry, and I'll never do it again. Just please don't. Please…" Her body lay on top of the bedding, her pussy still mine to take.

"If I begged you to stop, would you have stopped?"

She was silent since we both knew the answer.

"Cry all you want. I'll just enjoy it even more." I slid my cock farther inside, aroused by the moisture that met me.

"No! Please." She panted underneath me, desperation in her voice. "Don't do this. Don't do this to me. You're better than this."

I laughed even though she wasn't trying to be funny. "I'm definitely not better than this. I stole you, so I'm not above using you."

"Hit me. Break me. Kill me. Just please don't do this…"

Inexplicably, those words sank into me—right to the bone. She preferred death over sex, and that pulled at my misplaced compassion. The head of my cock was still inside her, feeling the wet moisture. "Why are you wet then, Lovely?" I didn't pull my dick out because it felt too incredible inside her. So soft. So warm.

She breathed heavily underneath me, her face pressed into my sheets.

"I asked you a question." I tightened my grip on her wrists and squeezed her neck.

She twisted her head, trying to free herself from the hold. "I'm attracted to you…"

My fingers immediately relaxed around her throat, those

words soothing on my ear. Her confession was so honest and so embarrassing. I was taking her against her will, and she still got wet for me. It truly was humiliating —for her.

"But I don't want this. Maybe my body does, but I don't. So have some compassion, and let me go."

My hand still clamped her wrists together, and I struggled to release her. Knowing she wanted my cock made me want to keep going. My attraction to her doubled within seconds. Now I wanted her sensually, her legs wrapped around my waist as we moved together in mutual passion.

Not like this.

I found the strength to release her and pull the tip of my cock out. The second my wet cock felt the air of my bedroom, he twitched in frustration. I didn't pull on a pair of boxers because I wasn't ashamed of my nakedness.

London breathed a sigh of relief when I let her go, but she still hid her face. Her ass was still in the air and her panties around her ankles.

I forced myself to look away because it just made me harder. "I suggest you get dressed and leave before I change my mind."

She snapped out of it and pulled her clothes back on. She refused to meet my gaze before she darted out of the room, forgetting to close the door behind her.

I sat at the edge of the bed and tried to make sense of what just happened. I had every right to fuck her. After all, she had just tried to kill me in my sleep—a coward's attempt. I owned her. She was my four-million-dollar collateral that I took from Joseph. If I wanted to fuck her, I could. If I wanted to snap her neck, I could.

I could do whatever I damn well pleased.

But something held me back. She begged me not to rape her, and somehow, I caved. I still wanted her, but I managed to step away. When she told me she was attracted to me, that gave me some form of satisfaction. Her body wanted me even if her mind loathed me.

That would have to be enough—for now.

I didn't see her the following day because she stayed in her bedroom the entire time. She was probably trying to avoid me after the ordeal in the middle of the night. I couldn't blame her. My cock was an inch inside of her, and all her body could do in response was get wet.

THE SCOTCH KING | 73

I was remembering the feel of her tight pussy around my head when Ariel walked in.

"The helicopter is arranged for this evening. He's bringing a few men along."

"That's fine." I never expected him to come alone. Very rarely did I go anywhere without protection.

"Also, Joseph Ingram is on the line."

My fingertips were resting on my lips, but I immediately pulled them away when I heard her announcement. My hand formed a fist. "What did he say?"

"Nothing. Just said he wanted to speak to you."

"He has a lot of nerve…"

"You did tell him not to save her. But you never said he couldn't contact you."

I was too angry to smile. "You're right…as usual."

"I'm surprised he still wants her back. She's insufferable, if you ask me."

"I'm surprised you would say that." I continued the conversation but considered what I would say to Joseph when I got on the line.

"Why?"

"You remind me of each other. Both spitfires."

Ariel rolled her eyes in an affectionate way. "He's on line one." She walked out, this time closing the door behind her.

I stared at the satellite phone sitting on my desk, the one I used for work that was synced to Ariel's line. I watched it for several heartbeats before I finally took the call. "Hello, Joseph." I planned to say as little as possible, forcing him to speak with just my silence. But he better cut to the chase because I had shit to do. It gave me some sick satisfaction that his sister was attracted to me despite the fact that she was my prisoner. I already felt like I had gotten my revenge with that alone.

"Hello, Mr. Donoghue."

Good start.

"I know you have London, and I haven't made any attempts to get her back."

Because you're a pussy.

"But I hope you'll reconsider letting her go."

"Why would I do that?" I stared at my watch, seeing the minute hand circle round and round.

"She's just an innocent girl."

"She's not a girl," I said with a laugh. "She's all woman."

Joseph fell silent at the implication of my words, the vein in his forehead probably throbbing.

"And it's not gonna happen. I've decided what to do with her. She'll be leaving in a few days. Where she'll go…not for me to know."

"What do you mean?" Instead of keeping his cool, Joseph's panic escaped in his tone.

"A friend of mine is coming to dinner tonight. He has a preference for slaves. I'm going to introduce her to him and tell him what her price is."

"Who?" Joseph demanded.

One sick son of a bitch. I was cold and cruel, but this man was something else entirely. He made me look tame. "Bones."

Joseph knew exactly who he was. Bones was known for his taste in women. He liked to use them, to break their legs and then chase them around his mansion. He was undoubtedly cruel, killing them once he grew bored. Then he would buy another slave…and the cycle continued. "Have mercy, Crewe…"

"He'll pay me the four million dollars you didn't. And then we'll be even."

"Come on, I'll do anything you want. Please don't do that to her. She's a good person…" His voice broke like he was on the verge of tears.

I had no sympathy for him. "Shouldn't have crossed me. I've told you that before."

"There has to be a compromise."

"Not when I know how much this bothers you. You know she'll be tortured every single day of her life until Bones finally kills her. That can sit on your conscience every second until you finally see her grave and know her suffering is over."

"I'll do whatever you want—"

"Good bye, Joseph." I hung up and tossed the phone aside, finished with Joseph Ingram forever. I would get my perfect revenge, and every person who heard the story would fear me. When I walked into a room, everyone would bow.

Because I was the scotch king.

6

LONDON

Crewe walked into my bedroom without knocking, his brown eyes gleaming with sinister intent. "I'm having a guest for dinner. I want your hair and makeup to be done. Ariel can do it for you if you need help."

There were so many things wrong with that sentence. "First of all, I can do it myself. Second of all, I don't want to. And thirdly, who the hell is coming to dinner all the way out here?"

"A friend of mine. I want you to meet him."

"Why?"

Crewe walked toward me as I sat on the couch. He

looked formidable in his suit. "Because I'm going to sell you to him."

"What?"

"Part of my plan. I'll offer you for four million dollars. He'll think about it for a while before he agrees."

"Well, I don't agree." Crewe wasn't the best man on the planet, but at least he didn't rape me when I asked him not to. I would much rather stay with him, even if he was evil, because that was better than going anywhere else. "I'm not going anywhere."

"You're my property," he said quietly. "You don't get a say in this. Do your hair and makeup or I'll make it happen."

This conversation was so overwhelming that I didn't even think of the last time we spoke. When his thick cock was inside me, and I confessed that I thought he was good-looking and attractive. I was humiliated those words had come out of my mouth, but this conversation was far worse. "No."

He stepped closer to me then grabbed me by the throat. "Do as I say. Or I will fuck you." After a terrifying glare, he released me. "When I return in thirty minutes, you better have done as I've asked. Or my cock is going in your ass." He slammed the door on the way out, making me jump out of my skin.

I did as he asked because I didn't know what else to do.

If I defied him, he would make good on his threat.

But if I didn't defy him, I'd have to meet a man who would potentially buy me.

Either way, I lost.

Crewe came back thirty minutes later, wearing jeans and a dark green t-shirt. His thick arms were on display, lean and toned with corded veins protruding from the skin. He had just shaved, so his chin was free of hair.

He looked at me with approval. "I'm a little disappointed. I was hoping you wouldn't listen to me."

I ignored the implication.

"Take off that dress."

"You didn't tell me what you wanted me to wear." I stood at the foot of the bed with heels on my feet. I found the outfit in the closet, along with the other clothes Crewe had bought for me.

"Because I don't want you to wear anything."

The blood drained from my face.

"Strip down to your panties. Now."

I'd already stripped for him once. I couldn't do it again, especially in front of a stranger who wanted to buy me for immoral reasons. "No."

"No, what?" His hand shot out to my neck.

I threw my elbow down so his fingers wouldn't squeeze me anymore. "I'm not taking off my clothes for anyone. If you don't like it, you'll just have to—"

He grabbed the fabric of my dress and ripped it with his bare hands. A long tear stretched down past my waist, my bra visible now that the material was falling apart. He yanked on it again until it was in two pieces. "You can leave the heels on. Lose the bra."

"Fuck you." I'd never been so degraded in my life, stripped and objectified because I was a woman and not a man. I spit in his face and tried to kick him in the nuts.

He blocked the hit then slapped me across the face. "Spit

on me again, and see what happens." His hand unclasped the back of my bra in one fluid motion. It fell down my arms and onto the floor.

How did my life turn into this? "You're better than this, Crewe."

"No, I'm not," he said coldly. "When someone fucks with me, I teach them a lesson. Now you can try to avoid this as much as possible, but you won't succeed. I have all the control. You have nothing."

It was the first time I wanted to break down in tears. It was the first time I wanted to weep. All hope left my body when I realized I truly was just a piece of property, cattle to be sold to the highest bidder.

"We're going to have dinner now. You don't have to eat. You don't have to talk. Just sit there." He grabbed me by the elbow and guided me into the grand dining hall. My tits were out in the open, and only my panties covered my virtue. I passed Finley in the hallway, but he had enough respect for me to not stare.

Crewe pushed me into a chair then scooted me in.

I immediately covered my chest, my lungs tightening with impending tears. "Don't do this to me. Crewe, please…"

"Lower your arms." He grabbed both of my wrists and pinned them down. "Every time you cover them during dinner, I'll backhand you." He leaned over the back of the chair until his mouth was pressed to my ear. "Accept your fate. That's all you can do at this point." He walked out of the room just as Finley announced his dinner guest.

"Sir, Bones is here."

What kind of name is Bones? The name alone made me shake. Whatever it implied was something I couldn't handle. Without even seeing his face, I knew I would be terrified of that man.

Crewe and Bones shared a few words about the weather then Bones discussed his life in Rome. They headed to the dining room, their voices growing louder. I sat there in just my underwear, tears burning behind my eyelids. Some man was going to stare at me all through dinner— like I wasn't human.

Bones walked inside, his face fair and his hair blond. He was large around the midsection, and the air around him was full of tense creepiness. When his eyes fell on me, I immediately covered my face, disgusted by his gaze.

Crewe's hand moved to my shoulder. "What did we talk about, Lovely?"

I refused to lower my hands, to allow this sick man to see me. He had a thick mustache and evil eyes. He eye-fucked me while he looked at me, having no shame in seeing me as a prisoner. He was more terrifying than I expected him to be.

Crewe slapped me like he'd promised. The back of his hand smacked across my cheek. He put a great deal of force into it, making my cheek redden on impact.

I lowered my hands.

"She needs a bit of training," Crewe said. "That's all."

"She's fascinating." Bones walked to me then leaned over, staring down at my body like he had every right to examine me. Then he extended a hand and cupped my tit.

I smacked his hand. "Don't you fucking touch me."

He pulled back his fist and slammed it into my face, making me cry out in pain. He pulled back to do it again.

Crewe steadied his hand. "One is enough, Bones. Why don't you take a seat, and we'll drink some of my finest scotch?" Crewe placed his body between us, protecting me with his size.

I shouldn't have felt grateful, but somehow, I was.

Bones moved to the other side of the table.

Crewe sat beside me and asked Bones about his weaponry business. Apparently, Bones manufactured illegal weapons and sold them to the highest bidders from all around the world. I wasn't sure what Crewe and Bones had in common, but it was obviously something.

Finley served dinner, but I didn't dare eat a bite. I felt sick to my stomach. The pain from my eye was excruciating. I knew I would wake up with a black eye tomorrow.

Bones and Crewe continued to talk about business, focusing on Crewe's experience in selling intelligence. They mentioned someone named Crow and his participation in selling weapons to their allies.

I was bored of the conversation but still terrified.

"So," Bones said as he spoke with his mouth full. "Did you bring her along just to tease me?"

"No," Crewe said. "This fine lady is for sale, actually."

"Is she now?" He stared at my tits again, still eating. "How much? I'd love to give her a go."

I wanted to hurl all over the table.

"Four million," Crewe said. "The price is non-negotiable."

"Four million? Are you out of your mind?" Food flew from his mouth as he spoke, looking oddly like a pig.

"She's worth every penny," Crewe said with conviction. "She's got the feistiness you crave. Just last night, she snuck into my bedroom and tried to bash my skull in with a rock."

Bones gave a hearty laugh, deep from within his throat. "She's got spunk… I like that." His blue eyes moved to me again, seeing right through my skin to my untainted soul. He wanted to take all of me, all the things I cherished.

"She's got one hell of a mouth on her too," Crewe continued. "It's one smartass comment after another."

"Even better," Bones said. "But that price is pretty high, I'm sure you can agree."

"Like you can't afford it." Crewe gave a charming smile, using his natural charisma even on men.

"Well, of course," Bones said. "But I spend my money wisely. I can get a nice whore for a fraction of the cost."

"I'm not a whore," I hissed. I was tired of being discussed

like I wasn't even there. They joked about my spitfire personality, but they didn't understand I was just trying to survive. What would they do if they were in a situation like mine? Give up?

Crewe patted me on the shoulder. "She's right. She's not. And that's why she's better. She was in medical school when I took her, so this will be her first rodeo. She'll need to be trained. She'll need to be broken. But that's where all the fun is, if you ask me."

Bones took another bite of his food and nodded. "You're right about that."

I twisted my shoulder, moving away from Crewe's touch.

Crewe let me get my way and returned his hand to his lap. "I'll give you a few days to think about it. But after the third day, I'll open up the bidding to others."

"I've got to ask, Crewe," Bones said. "Where does the price tag come from?"

"Glad you asked." Crewe drank his scotch before he continued. "You know Joseph Ingram?"

"Vaguely," Bones said. "Name sounds familiar."

"Well, this idiot paid me with counterfeit bills. He was stupid enough to think he could get away with it."

Bones groaned quietly, his form of a smile. "That's insulting."

"If he had succeeded with an intricate plan, I might actually have some respect for him," Crewe said with a shrug. "But he did something so amateur. Within five minutes, we knew we'd been taken for a ride."

"Maybe he thought you wouldn't be able to track him down," Bones suggested.

"Well, it only took us two days. We brought him and his men to my headquarters in Glasgow. After a good beating, he doubled the amount he owed me. But, obviously, he never paid up. I couldn't get the money from him. Instead, I took his sister." Crewe wrapped his arm around my shoulders. "He knows all the horrible things that will be done to her, and that's enough revenge. But I'm selling her for the price he owes me—two birds with one stone."

Bones nodded slowly then lifted his glass to Crewe. "I commend you, Crewe."

Crewe clinked his glass against his. "Thank you." He threw back his glass and poured the scotch down his throat.

Bones did the same. "Perfect punishment. But I need to

think about it. In the back of my mind, I can't stop thinking about the number of whores I could get for the same price. Now that I know her backstory, I'm much more enticed. I'll give her greater beatings just because I know someone is hurting for her." He stared at me, his cruel gaze piercing my skin. I could feel arousal leaking from his skin with all the unsaid things he wanted to do to me. "I'd love to break both of her knees and watch her try to crawl away. I'd love to break her arm and command her to serve me. But she won't last as long as the others. She'll be buried in the yard within a year."

I forced myself not to shake, not giving in to my fear while Bones was present. But I'd never been so scared in my goddamn life. The sobs pounded in my chest, and I was on the verge of fainting. This man was a monster, far worse than Crewe could ever be. All he ever did was slap me—and that was because I slapped him first. When I asked him not to fuck me, he listened. Crewe wasn't evil at all—not in comparison to Bones.

When Bones finally left the house, I dashed into my bedroom and covered myself with clothes, my body finally shaking with terror. I couldn't catch my breath because I was gasping too hard. If I had to submit to that psychopath, I'd kill myself.

That was the much better alternative.

Crewe walked into my bedroom without knocking. "That went well."

I'd normally respond with a smartass comment, but I didn't have it in me.

"He'll be here with the cash in three days."

"He said that?" My one hope was the price might be too high. I thought I would be too expensive to buy, especially if I wasn't going to last long.

"Yeah." Crewe stood with his hands in his pockets, still looking handsome despite the evil sale he'd just made. "He just needs to get the funds and travel back. When you're always on the move, it's hard to get your finances together."

I didn't care about the explanation. "Crewe...don't do this." I begged once before, and he listened. Maybe he would listen again. "Please."

He looked down at me, nearly bored.

"I'll get you the money, okay? Your debt will be paid."

"You've got four million dollars lying around?" he asked with a cruel smile.

"No, but I'll find it." I'd sell drugs if I had to. "You're selling me to get your revenge. Let me buy myself."

He shook his head. "Even if you had the money, I wouldn't take it. Giving you to a madman like Bones is part of the plan."

"No…" I felt tears bubble in my eyes, but they didn't escape. "I'm begging you." I moved to my knees on the floor. "Please don't let him take me. I know you have compassion. I know you have sympathy."

His eyes darkened the moment I got to my knees. "I don't."

"Yes, you do. I've seen it."

"The only reason why I didn't fuck you is because I didn't want to tamper with the goods. Your pleas have no effect on me."

I didn't believe that. Or perhaps I chose not to believe that. "I'll do anything. Don't give me to that psychopath. He's insane."

"That's the point," Crewe said coldly. "He's the craziest

man I've ever done business with—and that's saying something."

I brought my hands together, not caring about how pathetic I'd become. I was on the ground like a rat, but I didn't care. I'd do anything to save my life, to save myself from eternal suffering. "Crewe, there has to be something you want. I can give you anything you need. Anything." My meaning was clear. I never thought I would offer something like this, but I was willing to sleep with him just to avoid Bones. I'd take Crewe over Bones any day.

"There's nothing I want more than to make an example of my enemies." He walked around me, his hands still in his pockets. "You leave in three days. You can blame me all you want, but your brother is responsible for this. Blame him."

"Crewe, please—"

He slammed the door.

Unable to bottle it in any longer, I succumbed to my tears.

7

CREWE

She didn't come out of her room for meals or anything else. She stayed hidden away. Finley checked on her from time to time to make sure she didn't hang herself in the closet. I wouldn't blame her if she tried to take that avenue.

I would do the same thing.

While it was an unfortunate circumstance for her, I didn't feel any sympathy. That was how the world worked. Evil men would exploit you the second you let your guard down. She should have hidden herself better, left her guard up longer. If she took care of herself, I wouldn't have been able to find her.

So this was her mistake.

Bones would take her away, beat her senseless, and then kill her within eight months. When she left my house, it would be the last time I'd ever see her—the last time anyone would see her besides Bones. Her death would be just as painful as her remaining months of life.

But I still didn't give a damn.

The silent treatment wouldn't change my mind. She could starve herself all she wanted. She would just have less energy to resist Bones if she planned to fight him. Her silent protest had no effect on me. If anything, it was nice not having to listen to her bitch and complain.

Ariel walked into my office. "I just got off the phone with Bones. He said he'll be here tomorrow afternoon to collect his new purchase."

"Thanks for letting me know."

She lingered in the doorway. "That girl has a long road ahead of her."

"She does. But I hope you aren't going soft on me."

"I'm not." She crossed her arms over her chest. "I just wonder if she's strong enough to survive it."

I shook my head. "No one is. You know how crazy he is."

She nodded. "Well, if I don't see her before she leaves, wish her good luck for me."

I chuckled. "She's not speaking to me. I don't think she'll ever speak to me again."

Ariel shrugged. "You aren't much of a talker anyway." She winked before she shut the door.

I finished my work day, went for a run around the island and did my fitness routine, had dinner, and then read before I went to bed. London might come to my room again to kill me in my sleep, but I suspected she wouldn't. At this point, killing me wouldn't change anything. Bones would come to collect her regardless.

I lay in bed and stared at the ceiling, thinking of my next trip to Glasgow. I'd had enough alone time on this island. When I returned to the city, I would visit some of my regulars. Sex was something I craved, like any other man, but there were times when I didn't need it. But the urge always came back.

Three weeks without it had surged my libido.

The door opened and someone walked inside. I knew exactly who it was without confirmation. If she was here to kill me again, it was pointless. She would need a gun if she planned to overpower me.

I sat up in bed and stilled at the sight.

London untied her bathrobe and let it slide off her shoulders and onto the floor. She stood there naked, her tits perky with hard nipples. Her long legs reached up to her neck. She sauntered to the bed, her hips shaking as she walked. Her hair was done in curls and dark eye shadow was around her eyes.

She reached the bed then climbed on top, her smooth skin warm when it came close to mine.

I stared at her in infatuation, my cock hard and ready to go. A part of me wondered if this was a dream. She hated me earlier in the day. I doubted she had the urge to fuck me after what I did to her.

She straddled my hips and lowered her body directly onto my cock. My sensitive skin could feel the folds of her pussy, the soft flesh I would penetrate over and over. She massaged her tits and grinded against me, having the charms of a whore.

My hands moved to her hips, and I dug my fingers into her soft skin. "Lovely…" I sat up and brought one nipple into my mouth, sucking the hard flesh and tasting it. She tasted clean and smelled like a woman, flowery.

As I cherished her body, I figured out exactly what she

was doing. "Fucking you won't change my mind about tomorrow. I'm going to sell you to Bones no matter how good you are in the sack."

Her fingertips moved through my hair as she held me close. She arched her back so I could get more of her other nipple into my mouth. She spent the last two days hating me, and now it seemed like that never happened. "You might change your mind…" She craned her neck so her lips could reach my shoulder. She pressed wet kisses across the skin until she reached my neck. Her tongue moved up to my ear, where her heated breath filled my canal.

My hands explored her back, feeling the hard definition under her silky soft skin. Her shoulders were petite but possessed strength. I could feel her power under my fingertips. Even though I'd already seen her naked several times, it felt like a new experience. Now I was touching her, exploring her.

I moved forward and positioned her on her back, my hips moving between her thighs. My arms slid behind her knees, and I leaned over her, my cock rubbing against her folds. I stared down at her, my chest grazing against her perky tits. I eyed her lips with longing, seeing this beautiful woman underneath me.

When she first arrived here, I was unimpressed. She was just a woman like all the others, with soft hair and a curvy figure. She had emeralds for eyes and the attitude of a prison warden. But now I couldn't stop looking at her, seeing her as something else entirely. I recalled all the times she defied me, refusing to show fear even though she was terrified. Unwillingly, she made me respect her.

And that was a hard thing to accomplish.

She pressed her hands against my chest and slid her palms upward, rubbing both of my hard pectoral muscles. She reached my shoulders and dug her fingers into the skin, feeling the strength my body carried. Her legs tightened around my waist, her ankles hooking together.

I stared at her lips and anticipated the surge of adrenaline. Her lips probably tasted better than her skin. She had the confidence to be utterly sexy, to be my fantasy. The fact that she had crawled on top of me and outright asked for sex gave her the control.

But I liked giving it away.

Now she was pinned underneath me, ready for me to enjoy.

I pressed my mouth to hers and slowly kissed her, feeling a current surge through me the moment we touched. My arms shook from the ecstasy, the unexpected chemistry. I didn't want to fuck her right away. Kissing her provided enough satisfaction, enough heat. My tongue moved into her mouth until I found hers. They danced together slowly, our chemistry combustive and powerful. My cock slowly grinded against her folds, taking advantage of the moisture pooling between her legs.

Fuck.

I dug my hand into her hair and fisted the strands, feeling the power surge through me as I dominated her. She was mine willingly. I claimed her the second she gave me the opportunity. Now I didn't want to let her go. I wanted to kiss her forever, to feel the ache in my lips from wanting so much more.

She slowly dragged her nails down my back, nearly piercing the skin with the pressure. "Fuck me."

I growled into her mouth, feeling my cock twitch at the same time. I couldn't remember the last time I shared a scorching kiss like that, the last time I had a sexier woman than London underneath me. She begged for me, and I knew the plea was sincere because her pussy was soaked.

"Crewe…"

Now I really was lost. Nothing was sexier than a woman whispering my name. She had the charms of an experienced courtesan, like she had pleased men for a living. But she possessed the innocence to make her seem untouched, like a white flower in the middle of the forest —rare and beautiful.

She directed the head of my cock inside her then gripped my hips, her nails digging into me. Then she tugged, impatiently pulling me inside her.

I slid inside her, moving through her wet tightness with a loud moan. I sank deeper and deeper, getting every inch completely inside her until my balls tapped against her ass. I breathed through the pleasure, feeling like a king when I was inside this gorgeous woman. My mouth was pressed to hers as I breathed through the intoxication.

She moaned quietly, her nails digging into me harder. Her ankles remained ironclad around me. She breathed into my mouth with sexy sounds, enjoying the feel of my cock as much as I enjoyed the feel of her tight pussy.

"Fuck, you feel good." I thrusted into her slowly, sliding through her tightness as I patiently waited for her to acclimate to me. "Are you a virgin?" I waited for her answer, hoping it was yes.

"No. It's just been a while…"

That answer was just as good. I thrusted into her with my hand tightly wrapped around her hair. Every time I slid inside her, I was greeted by moisture that continued to pool for me. I pressed my face close to hers as I moved, wanting to do so many things at once. I wanted to suck her nipples into my mouth, finger her ass, and slap her across the face all at the same time.

But kissing her was just as good as all those other things.

There was something innately erotic about feeling our lips move together and our tongues graze across one another. Every time she took a breath, I sucked the air into my lungs, invigorated by her arousal. She'd seemed so plain when I first looked at her, but now, I found her to be the most erotic woman on the planet.

Her hands moved up my back and into my hair, her hips slowly grinding against me. She accepted my cock slowly, taking it in as she loosened up. She took my dick like a pro, as if the size and thickness didn't cause her much pain.

But I knew it did.

My desire took full control, and I pounded into her with more force, my balls slapping against her ass with every thrust. Sweat trickled down my chest as I continued to kiss and fuck her.

Damn, I already wanted to come.

I deepened the angle and rubbed my pelvic bone against her clit, enjoying the wetness against my skin. I applied the right pressure, wanting her to come. I shouldn't have cared about her pleasure, but the gentleman that I was, for the most part, wanted her to get the same experience I got. Besides, watching a woman come was just an extra turn on.

I continued to kiss her because I didn't want to stop. Her mouth was just as intoxicating as her cunt. I could do this all night. I loved having this woman underneath me, enjoying every inch of my cock ramming into her.

Her hands moved to my forearms, where her grip tightened. Her lips stopped moving, and she panted into my mouth, her nipples hardening to the tips of diamonds. "Crewe…" She could have been faking it, pretending to feel the exquisite pleasure just to manipulate me. But when her pussy suddenly constricted, tightening around my shaft with surprising force, I knew it was genuine.

Then she rolled her head back and moaned. Her sigh of pleasure turned into a scream, one that would echo around the house and even reach the first floor. Shit, the rats in the basement could hear it. She pulled me deeper into her as the moans trailed away.

"You enjoy that, Lovely?"

"Yes…" Her lips moved with mine again, her moisture flooding my length. Her tongue darted into my mouth, thanking me for the climax I just gave her.

I pumped into her harder, wanting to release inside that tight little cunt. My balls slapped against her ass as I worked my hips, getting ready for the finale. I wanted my seed to sit inside her all night long, my presence still within her long after I was gone.

Her tits bounced as I fucked her. "I'm not on the pill right now…" She knew I was going to come, must have felt how tight my cock became inside her. "I want your come but…"

Hearing that confession made my spine coil. I wanted to dump everything inside her, mounds and mounds of my seed until she was full to the brim. But coming on her tits wouldn't be so bad. They were gorgeous. And it would be fucked up to knock her up before I handed her over to Bones. Not very good etiquette.

I fucked her harder until I felt the orgasmic wave of

release. I pulled out of her just in time to come on her stomach and tits, creating white pools. I shot out far and got it everywhere, hitting her right in her cleavage as well as the surrounding skin. The sight gave me a second wave of desire while admiring my handiwork.

I kissed her again even though the fun was over. I was satisfied by the beautiful woman underneath me, covered in my come. My tongue darted into her mouth again, and my hand returned to her hair. The kiss lasted for minutes just because it felt good. She knew how to work her mouth, how to move her tongue in all the right ways. I'd even go as far as saying she was the greatest kisser I'd ever had been with.

I got off her then returned to the top of the bed where the pillows were. I lay on the sheets with the comforter kicked back, letting my body cool off because it was still covered in sweat. Exhaustion crept into my bones now that the fun was over.

London cleaned up in the bathroom before she joined me in bed, lying beside me.

I didn't open my eyes. "What are you doing?"

"Going to sleep," she whispered, her back to me.

"Not in here. Go to your room."

She didn't move, the sheets pulled to her shoulder.

Now my eyes opened, irritation coursing down my spine. "What did I just say?"

"You're really going to kick me out?"

I turned over, my mood souring. "Hooking up doesn't change anything. I'm not going to sleep with you. I'm selling your ass to Bones tomorrow. If you thought I would actually care for you after a good lay, you're an idiot."

8

CREWE

I didn't see London the next morning, but Finley assured me she was well.

She hadn't tried to kill herself in the middle of the night.

Ariel knocked on my open door. "Bones is an hour out."

"Thank you." In an hour, my prisoner would be gone forever. Joseph, along with the rest of the world, would know I made good on my threats. I unleashed unforgivable punishments on my enemies—something they could never forget.

"Anything you need me to do before I head home for the day?" she asked.

"No, that's it. Have a good night."

She smiled before she walked out.

I stared out the window to the green island beyond. The sky was pale blue, nearly white. The wind was light that afternoon, the storm off the coast of Ireland long gone. I admired the beauty of the outside world before I realized it was time to get London ready.

I walked into her bedroom without knocking since I owned her and the room. "Pack your things. He'll be here in thirty minutes."

She sat at the foot of the bed with her knees pulled to her chest. In a baggy shirt and sweatpants, she looked like she hadn't slept at all last night. Her eyes were directed out the window, a defeated gloss to her gaze.

"Did you hear me?" I asked with more force.

"I don't have any things because I'm not a person…"

I listened to the melancholy in her voice but didn't let it sink under my skin. I walked farther into the room until I was by her side. Then I grabbed her by the throat, surprised when she didn't show the slightest reaction. "Enough with the pity party."

"Why couldn't you just kill me?" Her voice broke, and

tears streamed down her face like an unexpected avalanche. "That's vengeance enough."

"But not good vengeance." I released my fingers from her throat, annoyed my touch had no effect on her. "Forget your tears, and get over it."

She looked up at me, her cheeks stained with tears she'd already shed. I'd never witnessed her cry before even though she'd struggled the entire time she lived there. Like diamonds, her tears sparkled. They caught the natural sunlight from the window and twinkled. Just when old tears streaked down and dripped off her cheek, new ones developed. "Please don't do this, Crewe. There's still time."

All I did was shake my head.

She grabbed my wrist and squeezed it. "I know you're a good man. I know you're better than this."

I watched new tears well up inside her eyes before they bubbled and dripped out. Her fingers wrapped around my wrist just the way she gripped my arms when we were in bed the night before. Something shifted inside me, a feeling I couldn't identify. I wasn't even sure if it was good or bad. "I'm not a good man. I take intelligence from friends and allies, and I sell it to their enemies for a profit. I'm not better than the law since I refuse to obey it. I live by my own rules, my own moral code. If I want to sell you, I will. I don't give a damn if you're an innocent woman trying to save lives. To me, you're just a pawn in a game. Your suffering and your death mean absolutely nothing to me." I twisted my hand from her grasp. "Nothing."

I sat on the couch and watched the minutes tick by. The large hand of the grandfather clock moved round and round, marking down to the moment when Bones would land on the field outside my home.

I sipped my scotch, feeling the ice cubes press against my lips as I drank. When the glass was empty, I refilled it and rested it on my knee, staring at the clock again. London had stopped sobbing fifteen minutes ago. Even with her door closed to her bedroom upstairs, I could still hear her cries.

They annoyed me.

Finley entered the room. "Sir, the helicopter has just landed. Bones will be here shortly."

I raised my glass to him. "Thanks, Finley."

He nodded and left.

I abandoned my drink and rose to my feet, adjusting my tie without seeing myself in a mirror. I placed my hands in my pockets and walked to the front door. "London, get your ass down here." I'd give her a second to take a breath before she walked downstairs to be claimed by this madman. But if she waited too long, I'd walk up there and drag her down by her hair.

Finley opened the front door and ushered Bones and his two cronies inside.

"Always a pleasure." I shook Bones' hand.

"Likewise. And where's my little pleasure?" He wore a gray suit with a black tie, standing at my height but with much more fat around the middle.

"She's coming."

"Excellent." Bones handed a suitcase to me. "It's all in there."

While Bones was evil, he wasn't a cheat. If he said the money was in there, I knew he was good for it. "Thank you." I set it down beside me.

Bones extended his hand again, and one of his cronies pulled a chain from a bag. It was black and heavy, and at the end was a collar meant to bind around someone's neck. It was old and rusty, probably worn by other slaves he'd had before London. He opened the collar and separated the two pieces of metal, ready to wrap it around her neck.

He was going to have her on a leash for the entire ride to Rome.

I stared at the metal and thought about all the things he would do to her, about the way he'd already punched her in the face and given her a black eye. Bones was big and strong. London didn't stand a chance against him.

Memories from last night flooded my mind—the scorching kisses she gave me and how tight her pussy was. Bones would never give her that kind of sex, the merciful kind. It would only be chains, whips, and broken bones.

I actually felt sorry for her.

"What's taking her so long?" Bones asked with a sigh. "I should be getting back. Besides, I'm eager to play with my new toy." He grinned in a sickening way, one eye smaller than the other. His teeth were crooked, and he smelled like old garlic.

I looked at the chain again, feeling uneasy.

"Crewe," Bones said with a growl. "Did you hear me?"

I came back to the conversation, still utterly confused. I didn't have a clue what was happening to me. All I could think about was London hopping on one foot as she tried to run from Bones with her other leg broken. She would be tortured every single day, unable to sleep because she would be so terrified. If he didn't kill her, she would die from a heart attack.

Or she would kill herself.

For the first time in my life, pity rose in my heart.

"I'm sorry you've come all this way, but I've changed my mind." I couldn't stop staring at the metal collar, wondering how heavy it would feel once it sat on London's shoulders. "I'll compensate you for your trouble."

Bones raised an eyebrow, his rage burning under the skin. "Is this a joke, Crewe?"

"I'm afraid not." I snapped my fingers. "Finley, retrieve the yellow envelope in my desk drawer."

"Right away, sir." Finley darted down the hallway and disappeared.

"Was this all a sick game?" Bones demanded. "I didn't realize you were the stupid type."

I moved the briefcase to his feet, returning the money. "It was never a game. I've just realized how she could be better suited." Finley returned with the envelope and handed it to me. "But I'm compensating you one million for wasting your time. I understand you're a busy man." I dropped it into his hand.

His anger disappeared once he felt the wad of cash.

"I'm sure there will be no hard feelings." It was the easiest million he would ever make in his life.

Bones handed it to one of his cronies and silently asked him to count it.

I pretended not to be offended.

"What are you going to do with her?" Bones finally asked.

"Not sure. Might keep her for my own entertainment."

Bones didn't smile, but he no longer seemed jovial. "Can't blame you." He grabbed the suitcase and handed it off to one of his men. "Good evening, Crewe. Until next time."

I followed him to the door. "Until next time." I watched him walk out and return to the helicopter far away on the field. Clouds covered the sky and it looked like it might rain. In fact, it would probably pour. I felt the cool air brush against my skin, and I wondered exactly what I had done. I'd risked pissing off one of my greatest allies—all for one woman. That conversation could have gone much worse. He could have declared war on me, making me an enemy for wasting his time. Somehow, I got lucky. If I hadn't given him that cash, things could have ended quite differently. Instead of making back the money Joseph owed me, I lost more of it.

How the fuck did that happen?

9

LONDON

I couldn't go down there.

My legs refused to move. I couldn't hold my own weight. I hadn't left the bed since Crewe walked out. The tears came and went. Just when they stopped, they'd start back up again. My chest carried a permanent ache that wouldn't go away.

I considered jumping out the window and trying to break my neck. But from the second story, it just wasn't high enough. Crewe seemed like a man with guns in the house, but I hadn't found any.

How did my life come to this?

The day before I was dragged out of my bed in the

middle of the night, I had just finished my rotation on the surgical floor. I was fascinated by my patients, genuinely concerned for their recovery and their lives. I felt a high, a rush from doing something meaningful.

Now I was here—about to become a slave.

Crewe walked into the bedroom, his brown eyes nearly black in anger. He called up to me twice, but I still didn't obey. I wasn't scared of his wrath, just in shock over what was about to happen.

"You'll have to drag me out..." I tightened my arms around my waist and waited for his attack. "But I'll fight you the whole way, kicking and screaming. And when Bones has me, I'll do the same to him."

Crewe slowly approached me, still looking down at me with a slight sneer. "New plan."

I stared at him, my breathing all over the place. "What?"

"I sent Bones away because I've come up with a better idea, a better punishment."

What punishment could possibly be worse than being that madman's prisoner?

"You're mine—forever." He stared at me like he hated me, like I'd done something terrible to him within the past hour. "You're my prisoner, my slave. You'll do as I ask without me having to ask more than once. I'll wear you on my arm everywhere I go, so everyone will know what I've done to Joseph Ingram."

My arms dug into my waist as I gripped myself tightly. It seemed like I was missing a piece of the puzzle because this wasn't adding up. I voluntarily slept with Crewe, obviously with an ulterior motive, but that was something I couldn't have done with Bones no matter how hard I tried. Bile wouldn't stop rising up my throat. From what I could see, being forced to do whatever he wanted was far better than going home with that asshole who gave me a black eye.

"You'll never go home. You'll never escape. This is your life until you die or I kill you myself." His hand moved to my neck, squeezing me tightly. "Do you understand me?" When I didn't answer fast enough, he gripped my chin and forced me to look at him. "Do you?"

All I could feel was relief. I never thought being Crewe's prisoner would be a blessing, but in comparison to my previous fate, it was welcomed. Crewe was complicated and sinister, but he wasn't evil like that other man. It actually seemed like I had a second chance at life, something to live for. "Yes."

He released my chin.

"But I'll never stop trying to escape. I'll never obey your commands. I'll never act like a dog. The only thing I accept is being your prisoner, but that doesn't mean I'm a willing prisoner."

That must have been enough because Crewe walked out.

When the door was shut, I cried again. But this time, they were tears of relief. I was so grateful that my heart was about to explode. It was the first surge of joy I'd had since I arrived here, and even though it was pathetic to be grateful for something so miserable, it didn't change anything.

The tears fell.

I slept well for the first time in three days.

Nightmares didn't haunt me. Bones didn't assault me, grabbing my tits while he threw his head back and laughed. He didn't break my bones or chase me with a baseball bat. All I dreamt of were the seals that swam along the coastline, sleeping on rocks until they accidentally rolled over and plummeted into the water.

The next morning, I woke up feeling refreshed—and grateful.

I walked into the kitchen, my stomach rumbling. I couldn't remember the last time I'd eaten. I didn't have much of an appetite for the past three days. My stomach was tied up in tense knots.

When I rounded the corner, I saw Crewe standing there. He was in a black t-shirt with matching running shorts. A line of sweat stained the fabric of his shirt around the neck, suggesting he'd just gone for a run. He sipped his coffee and looked out the window, seeming to be lost in his thoughts.

When I slept with him, I wasn't to admit I enjoyed it. He was a very attractive man, dark and mysterious. While my mind was repulsed by him, my body didn't feel the same way. As stupid as it was, I held a soft spot for him. He could have done whatever he wanted to me that one night. I had every intention of killing him, and even though he knew that, he still let me go.

I didn't think he was as evil as he claimed to be.

No other man would have stopped what they were doing. The head of his cock was already inside me. My hands were pinned to my back, and he had a tight grip on my neck. There was nothing I could have done to get out of that hold.

But he let me go.

Crewe was still my enemy, so I couldn't go soft on him. If I ever had the opportunity to escape, I would take it. If it ever came down to him or me, I knew I would pick myself in a heartbeat.

But I was still a woman.

My plan was to soften him up, to make him want me enough that he wouldn't hand me over to Bones. If I made myself valuable to him, he would want to keep me. I wasn't entirely sure if my plan had worked or not. After we slept together, he didn't seem to have any affection toward me. In fact, it seemed like he hated me even more. His decision to change the punishment may have been coincidental, having something to do with Bones or the circumstance. I would never know because he would never tell me.

He must have seen me in the reflection of the glass because he spoke. "Sleep well?"

"Like a rock."

He sipped his coffee and continued to stare out the

window. He didn't say anything else, still quiet in his repose.

Finley emerged from the kitchen, wearing a white chef jacket that went over his collared shirt and slacks. "I was just about to make breakfast for Mr. Donoghue. Would you like anything, Lady London?"

My stomach growled in response. Thankfully, I was the only one who heard it. "Please. I'll eat anything."

Crewe sipped his coffee again. "I'm glad you've finally changed your attitude. Most people would take advantage of having a personal chef."

Finley ignored his master's comments. "You'll need to be more specific, Lady London. Because I can make anything." He gave me an affectionate smile, warm in contradiction to Crewe's coldness. He had wrinkles around his eyes, but they somehow made him comforting. He was the only person who was remotely nice to me here.

I should take advantage of that more often. "I'll have whatever Mr. Donoghue is having."

Crewe turned around and finally looked at me, the front of his shirt coated in sweat. "Call me Crewe—that's it."

He stared me down, daring me to defy him in front of his butler. "Nothing else."

All I did was nod.

"Mr. Donohue likes egg whites with a side of grilled greens," Finley explained. "Would you like that as well?"

I couldn't stop myself from cringing. "Yuck, absolutely not. Who the hell eats that for breakfast?"

"A man who looks like this." He moved his hand across his rock-hard abs, making a point.

I rolled my eyes. "Arrogance isn't sexy."

"I'm confident," he corrected.

"Confidence is quiet," I argued. "And you aren't quiet."

Instead of being angry, the corner of his lip rose in a smile. "You're cute when you're a smartass."

Both of my eyebrows rose. "Are you flirting with me?"

"No. If I were flirting with you, you'd be bent over the kitchen table by now." The corner of his mouth was still raised in a smile, but his eyes smoldered with intent.

My cheeks flushed since Finley was standing right there, listening to all of this.

Finley spoke as if he didn't hear a single thing. "Then what would you like, Lady London?"

"You can just call me London." The title was unnecessary.

"No," Crewe interrupted. "You're to call her Lady London."

Finley didn't object.

But I did. "If I want to be addressed by my name, that's how I'll be addressed."

"Not in this house," Crewe threatened. "I own everything under this roof—including you."

I shot him a disgusted look. "You're a real piece of work, you know that?"

"Would you say I'm better than Bones?" he countered. "Because I'll gladly hand you over to him if that's where you want to be." He covered up his smile by sipping his coffee.

Now I really hated him.

"What will it be, Lady London?" Finley asked. "I can whip up anything, especially American delicacies."

The thought of food made me forget Crewe. "Can you make pancakes?"

"The fluffiest pancakes in the world," Finley said with a smile. "Anything else?"

"Bacon and eggs?" I asked hopefully. "Maybe some toast?"

"Of course. Coming right up." Finley pulled items out of the fridge and got to work. "Have a seat and drink some coffee."

I moved to a chair at the table and cupped the mug with my hands, feeling the warmth.

Crewe continued to lean against the counter as he stared at me. "That's a big appetite for one person."

"Not when you haven't eaten in three days."

He chuckled under his breath and took a seat across from me at the table. I preferred this table to the one in the other room, where I sat naked and Bones grabbed my tits like he already owned my body without paying for it. Crewe sipped his coffee and stared at me head-on, his gaze dark and intimidating. I felt like I was being stripped naked with just his expression.

I refused to be intimidated by this man. I didn't believe

he was as dangerous as he claimed. He never hurt me unless I gave him a reason to, and he did listen to me if I begged enough. I was actually grateful to be sitting across from him right now—and not that other man.

Finley placed the dishes on the table. "Enjoy." He left the room and gave us privacy. Crewe's small plate was unremarkable, just eggs and vegetables.

That wasn't breakfast.

I dumped syrup on my pancakes then took a bite of bacon, feeling the crunch between my teeth. Without thinking, I moaned at the taste, my stomach on the verge of ecstasy.

Crewe watched me, partially smiling. "I've never seen a woman eat like that."

"Like what?" I asked. "Like a real person who eats food? Do you only spend time with supermodels?"

He grinned. "There it is again."

"What?" I grabbed my fork and cut into my eggs.

"The tone of jealousy." He set his coffee down and grabbed his fork.

"What?" I asked incredulously. "I'm not jealous."

"You obviously picture the kind of women I sleep with and assume they must be supermodels. And you're right. I've never slept with a woman who wasn't absolutely stunning." He took a bite of his food and stared me down while chewing, his jaw working silently.

I knew he purposely complimenting me, but I refused to be flattered. "The only woman I'm jealous of is Ariel—because she gets to go home every day."

"But she's never truly off the clock. She works from home a lot."

"Doing what?" I didn't totally understand what Crewe did for a living. He said he sold intelligence, but what did that mean, exactly? He didn't seem to be a government official to any particular country.

"A lot of things. She's the biggest cog in my machine." He took another bite, nearly finishing his food because his meal was so small. "Wouldn't know what to do without her."

"Now I am a little jealous."

He smiled. "I figured. You're the jealous type."

"I'm jealous that you respect her so much, but you don't show me any respect." This man obviously wasn't as much of a pig as he claimed to be. Ariel wasn't a slave under his orders. She was free to do whatever she wanted, and he obviously trusted her.

"Why would I show you any respect if you haven't earned it?"

"Excuse me?" Both of my eyebrows rose. "I've been locked up here for weeks, and I haven't had a break down or killed myself. You bet your ass I deserve some respect."

He sipped his coffee, not seeming to care about what I just said. "It takes a lot more than that to impress me, Lovely."

I wanted to ask him to stop calling me that, but it was pointless. "So, what now? You're just going to keep me here forever?"

"Among other things," he said vaguely.

"What's that supposed to mean?"

"How about you don't worry your pretty little head over it?" He cut into his greens and took a few bites.

"I'm not some airhead. You must have some idea of what you're going to do with me. I deserve to know."

"Your sense of entitlement confuses me." He chewed slowly, drawing out the seconds between speaking. "I told you that you're my property now—indefinitely. You do as I ask when I ask you to do it. Your life is no longer your own. So you don't deserve anything."

I wanted to strangle him. Just that morning, I was grateful he didn't let Bones take me away. But now I wanted to kill him all over again.

"Once you accept that, you'll come to appreciate the opportunity you've been given."

"Opportunity?" I practically gagged the word out. "You consider slavery to be an opportunity?"

He swallowed, his throat shifting in the process. His chin was covered with thick stubble, and it reached down his throat. "I'm one of the most powerful men in the world. I'm richer than most countries. You're never more safe or more wealthy than you are when you're with me. You can have anything you could possibly dream of."

"That's useless if the one thing I want is freedom."

"Freedom is overrated," he said coldly. "You think paying a massive amount in student loans just to get an education is freedom? You think being taxed a ridiculous amount every year while you save lives is freedom? You think living in a country where you'll always be deemed less qualified than a man is freedom?" He shook his head slightly. "There's a lot more to life than that, Lovely. I can show you the world. I can show you things you can't even conceive of in that smart brain of yours. Instead of bitching and complaining all the time, shut up and appreciate what's right in front of you."

10

CREWE

Ariel walked into my office in jeans and a gray blouse. She had elegant taste, wearing clothing that made her both respectable and beautiful. Her hair was pulled back into a loose bun and her eye makeup made the blue color of her irises stand out. "Had a change of heart?" She lowered herself into the chair in front of my desk and crossed her legs.

I set down the document I was reading. "Realized I could put her to better use."

"Really?" She cocked her head, her beautiful face looking ice-cold. "You found a better revenge than handing her over to one of the cruelest men in the world? If so, I'd like to hear what it is."

Ariel had known me for a long time, so it was difficult to avoid her detection. Her gaze was sharper than a microscope. She could see things far below the surface. She could spot my emotions before I even expressed them.

It was fucking annoying.

"If I keep her on my arm, everyone will know I stole her from Joseph. And I have no problem parading that in front of the goddamn world. He'll be forced to do nothing —like the coward that he is."

"Really?" She rested her arms on the armrests. "What about the four million dollars you're missing?"

"I'll get it back."

"How?" she demanded.

I didn't like being challenged, not even by her. "Don't you have work to do?"

"Yes, a lot of it." She straightened in the chair. "But I'm not going to let my boss, the man in charge of everything I've worked so hard to grow, go soft on that little fucking whore. Don't insult me with your excuses. I know exactly what you did, Crewe. So don't pretend I'm some kind of idiot."

Her fire always impressed me. Somehow, she intimidated even the most frightening men. In a lot of ways, she reminded me of my new prisoner with her zero tolerance for bullshit. Ariel got work done on a time crunch, never letting anything stand in her way. The fact that she could play a man's game and succeed always got my attention. When I saw her hold her own against five brutal men, I offered her a job on the spot.

"What the hell were you thinking, Crewe? Joseph spat in our faces when he tried to undercut us, and this is your retaliation? This is how we handle our problems now?"

"Enough." I raised my hand, effectively silencing her. Ariel was one of the few people who could call me out on my bullshit. But she couldn't insult me beyond that. "When Bones walked in with that chain and collar, I changed my mind. I knew what he was going to do to her, and I couldn't go through with it. I'm not going soft, alright? Keeping her as my prisoner will be punishment enough. Joseph will know exactly what I'm doing with her every night. That'll definitely give him nightmares."

Ariel pressed her lips tightly together in annoyance, but she didn't insult me again. "Are you fond of her or something?"

"Absolutely not." I found her intelligence and wit

entertaining, but that was it. She was an entitled brat who thought she could always get her way. She was such an idiot she actually thought she could outsmart me. She was just a pretty face with a curvy body—nothing more.

Ariel narrowed her eyes like she saw something in my expression. "Did you fuck her?"

Lying wasn't in my nature. I could bend the truth sometimes, but when asked a question outright like that, there was no wiggle room. So I didn't say anything at all, which was good as an admission of guilt.

She hid her displeasure at the news. "If you wanna screw your prisoner, I couldn't care less. But don't let it be anything more than that."

"It's not."

"It obviously is if you changed your mind about Bones. You're one of the harshest men I've ever met. I've never seen you reconsider a punishment, no matter how cruel it was. Don't change. I admire your coldness and don't want it to disappear."

"It won't. You don't need to worry."

Ariel finally let it go. "What are you going to do with her, then?"

"I already told you."

"When she's not making appearances as your slave."

"She'll service me in my free time." Discussing my sex life with Ariel didn't bother me. I felt like I was talking to one of the guys, someone who understood my sexual appetite without judgment. She rarely discussed hers, but that was because she didn't have much time for dating in her line of work. "That'll be punishment enough."

"I thought you already slept with her?"

"She seduced me so she could manipulate me into not handing her over to Bones."

Ariel glared at me.

"And it didn't work. I changed my mind for my own reasons. The sex had nothing to do with it."

"You expect me to believe that?"

"Yes, if you want to keep your job."

She rolled her eyes and stood up. "This place would fall apart without me, and you know it." She walked to the door, carrying herself with grace. She was a beautiful woman, but she blended in with the boys at the same time.

I smiled when her back was turned. "No, it wouldn't fall apart. Finley would replace you."

She laughed and turned around. "What's he gonna do? Cook all the problems away?"

I shrugged. "He could cook people. I've seen it done before."

She continued to laugh as she walked out. "I better step up my game. I'm about to be replaced."

London spent most of her time outside. She walked around the island with her binoculars and explored, watching the wildlife and looking at the indigenous plants that were native to the Shetland Islands. Even on the coldest days, she still went outside for most of the afternoon. Only when it rained did she stay inside the house.

I'd been busy with work, so I didn't pay much attention to her. Sometimes her abrasive comments annoyed me, her little-know-it-all attitude getting under my skin. Even after being here for a month, she still hadn't conformed to her new living arrangement. She had this ridiculous notion that she would eventually escape.

I'd expected to break her by now. But it was going to be more of a challenge.

Oh well. I like challenges.

I sat in the living room and read a book while the fire cracked in the hearth. A TV was mounted on the old stone wall, but I hardly ever watched it. TV and film bored me. Telling a story in such a rushed amount of time always diluted its power. But with a book, there was never any end.

London announced her presence with her light footsteps. She sat on the other couch, in a pair of black leggings and a pink sweater. Dunbar brought her clothes on his return trips to the island, and he outfitted her with clothing that clung to her curves perfectly. Her hair was pulled back into a ponytail, and I kept picturing my hand fisting it as I shoved my cock into her mouth. Now that days had passed, I was eager to fuck her again. Without even trying, she had a naturally beautiful face. Her green eyes sparkled like emeralds in a treasure chest. Her fair skin reddened easily under my palm. I wondered if her ass would have the same reaction.

I kept the book open on my lap. "Can I help you with something?"

"Am I not allowed to sit here?" she asked like a smartass. "I thought the house was open to me."

Every time she talked back to me, I wanted to slap her then fuck her senseless. Something about her seriously turned me on. Usually, if anyone ever disobeyed me, they were executed. I needed power and control at all times, and on the rare occasion I didn't get it, I was livid. But with her, it just made my attraction grow. I wanted to do more than just fuck her. I wanted to spank her then fuck her in the ass. I'd already had her once before, and my cock always hardened at the memory. She wasn't just good in bed. She was an amazing kisser. "Shut your mouth, or I'll shove my cock in there and do it for you." It wasn't an idle threat. Any excuse to fuck her mouth was a good one.

Her eyes narrowed in a glare, but she didn't say a word.

I turned back to my book, ignoring her on the other couch despite how hard my cock was. While I was a sexual man, I wasn't obsessed with women. They came and went, pleasing me and then disappearing. It took a lot to grab my full attention. Since I was thirty-two and it had never happened before, I assumed it would never happen.

But London made me reconsider.

"I never see you drink anything but scotch and coffee."

I didn't take my eyes off the page. "Because everything else tastes like shit."

"Even water?" she asked incredulously.

"Absolute piss."

"Do you like wine?"

I finally shut my book, knowing this conversation wasn't going to end. "What's with the questions, Lovely?"

Her face reddened in annoyance at the nickname, but she didn't bother correcting me. "I haven't spoken to anyone in three days. I'm bored and lonely."

"If you're lonely, I can fix that." I gave her a meaningful look, telling her exactly what I could do to make her feel less alone. I wanted a replay of the action we already had, the awesome sex that made me explode.

She rolled her eyes at my offer. "I'll pass."

"Seemed to enjoy it last time."

"I was faking it."

A laugh escaped my chest. "Yeah, sure…"

"I was," she repeated.

"Your mouth can lie, but your pussy can't. I made you come, and you know it."

Redness tinted her cheeks, the embarrassment shining through. She didn't deny the claim again, knowing it would just make her look worse.

"And I can do it again…" I drank my scotch, feeling the ice cubes press against my lips.

"No, thanks." She crossed her arms over her chest and purposely looked at the fire, not making eye contact with me.

I picked up on the hesitance in her voice and her lack of conviction.

Minutes ticked by and neither one of us said anything. I refilled my glass of scotch then poured her a glass. I set it on the coffee table in front of her. "You like scotch?"

"I'm not a big drinker. Maybe wine here and there…" She clung to the new conversation desperately, thankful that awkward talk was officially over.

"Give it a try."

She didn't object and took a drink. She didn't make a

sour face or struggle to swallow it. The amber liquid went down her throat and straight to her belly. I pictured pouring the scotch on her stomach and licking it off. She set the glass down again, half empty. "Not bad."

"Not bad?" I asked with a laugh. "That's the smoothest scotch you'll ever taste."

"Are you a fan?"

"Something like that." I turned back to the fire, watching the flames dance and pop. Life in Fair Isle was a welcomed break from the rest of the world, of the nonsense and the chatter, and I enjoyed my solitude more than the average person. London was obviously different, but she would get used to it. "What would you be doing if you were home right now?" The question came out of nowhere, my interest in this woman misplaced.

"Probably studying," she said as she looked into the fire. "By the way, people are going to be looking for me. I've never missed a day of class, and I have a lot of friends who will search everywhere to find me. It's only a matter of time before the police or Joseph track me down."

I almost felt bad for stomping on her dreams. "Good luck to them." I drank my scotch, letting the fire move down my throat. I rested the cool glass against my temple, letting the temperature cure the slight migraine that thudded behind my eyes.

She must have picked up on my tone because she released a sigh. "They're never going to find me, are they?"

"Let's just say, I'd be shocked if they did." I was untraceable. And if I wasn't, most governments were too scared of me to retaliate. It was easier to let my minor crimes slide than risk open warfare.

Her voice trailed away. "It's been four weeks…I thought Joseph would come for me by now. I guess he's not going to…"

A part of me wanted to tell her the truth, that I threatened to kill her if he made an attempt to rescue her. But the other part of me wanted to withhold that information and make her lose all hope. She would conform quicker, obey me faster. "You'll make a home here, Lovely. It won't be as bad as you think it will."

"Easy for you to say. How would you feel if I abducted you and forced you to live with me?"

I smiled at the fantasy. "I think it'd be pretty fun, actually."

She sighed in annoyance. "Do you ever think of anything else besides sex?"

"When I'm around you, no." I set the glass on the table then moved to her couch. I sat beside her, dangerously close. My arm draped over the cushion, resting against the back of her neck. She immediately took a quick breath at my unexpected hostility. My hand moved to her toned thigh and I gave it a gentle squeeze. My lips moved against her ear and I gave her a warm breath, arousal obvious in the way I cornered her against the arm rest on the couch. I wanted to fuck her right then and there, even if Finley walked inside. "It's all I ever think about." I kissed the shell of her ear and slowly moved my kisses down her neck, tasting her skin and sucking it into my mouth. My lips ached for more, feeling on fire every time I touched her. My hand moved up her thigh, and I listened to her breaths quicken as I touched her, feeling her mutual arousal.

She tilted her chin back slightly, and her hand dug into my hair. Quiet pants escaped her lips, her desire bubbling to the surface. Her smell washed over me, flowers and summer.

I lowered her to the couch, climbing on top of her as my mouth moved to hers. I sealed my lips against hers, moving them together with purposeful kisses. Before my tongue delved into her mouth, her tongue entered mine. Her hands moved to my shoulders and then my back, our make out session becoming heavier with every passing second.

My cock pressed against the front of my jeans, eager to be inside that tight pussy. The second the sex was over, I'd have to arrange for London to get the shot so I could come in her as much as I wanted. Coming on her tits would be enough for tonight.

I didn't break our kiss as I undid the top of my jeans with a single hand. My cock needed to come free. A drop formed on the tip and soaked through my boxers. Her pussy was probably just as wet, desperate to feel my rock-hard length.

But then she stopped the kiss. "No." She pushed me off her then rolled off the couch, falling to her knees before she stood once again.

My rage immediately came to the surface. No one told me no.

Ever.

"What do you think you're doing?" I whispered. "Get

back here. Now." If she defied me, I had no problem pinning her on her stomach with her ass in the air.

"No." She crossed her arms over her chest like she was naked and trying to hide herself from my sight. "I only fucked you to save myself. I'm not doing it again."

"Sure seemed like you enjoyed it."

"Whether I did or didn't, I don't want it." She turned to walk away.

I got to my feet instantly, grabbed her by the neck and threw her on the couch. "There's nowhere to run. Nowhere to hide. I get what I want, so just accept it. But if you fight, I won't mind. Bigger turn-on anyway." I yanked on the back of her leggings and pulled them off, revealing her perky ass.

She tried to buck me off. "I don't need to run or hide. You won't do it."

I released a dark laugh. "You don't know me very well."

"I do know you." She continued to fight underneath me. "Maybe you do evil things, but I know you won't do this. I know if I ask you to stop, you'll stop. I'm not afraid of you." She stared at me over her shoulder, looking incredibly sexy with her pants pulled down and her ponytail loose. "Did you hear me, Crewe? I'm not afraid of you. So get off me so I can go to bed."

I stared her down, my expression hardening. I didn't move my weight off of her, but I didn't move forward either. Her words pissed me off and placated me at the exact same time. She was calling my bluff, and I wanted to prove her wrong. But she was right, I didn't think I could do it. I did a lot of evil things on a daily basis, betrayed people's confidences and murdered men who deserved it. But no, I'd never forced myself on a woman before, even though I felt entitled to do it now.

She wanted me.

If I stuck my fingers in her pussy, I would be greeted with slick wetness. She couldn't kiss me like that unless she felt the same attraction. She wanted me.

But she still said no.

My body obeyed her command, and I moved off her, my cock still hard in my unbuttoned jeans.

She pulled her pants up then got off the couch. She moved around to the other side so the furniture was in between us. She didn't give me a gloating look. She didn't look relieved either. Her feelings were a mystery, actually. "You know what I think?" she whispered. "You aren't as evil as you claim. I think you have a heart somewhere in there—buried deep down inside."

"Trust me, I'm evil." Just because I wouldn't force her to sleep with me didn't mean I was a good person. I committed plenty of crimes on a daily basis. I've killed men just for getting in my way. "And I don't have a heart."

"I'm calling your bluff, Crewe," she said with confidence. "I don't know who you are. But I think I'm beginning to find out."

I had more to say, but I kept my mouth shut. Getting women had never been a struggle for me. All I did was turn on the charm, buy them a few drinks, and I usually got them in my sheets within the hour. I'd never had to resort to force to get my dick wet. But then again, I'd never met a woman I wanted this much who didn't want me. "Lovely, you aren't going to like what you see."

11

LONDON

I didn't know Crewe very well, but at least now I knew I was safe. One of my biggest fears as a woman was being taken against my will. The violent act was so sinister and dirty, marking my body and mind permanently. It didn't matter how many showers I took, the past would never wash off.

But Crewe would never do that to me.

When I slept with him the first time, I didn't know what else to do. I had to give him a reason to keep me, to give him a connection that would make him feel some fondness for me. Sex was the way to a man's heart if food wasn't an option.

So I did what I had to do.

But it was my choice. I had all the power and the control. I was attracted to him, so I did enjoy it. But despite my continued attraction to him, he was still the man keeping me captive. I wasn't going to sleep with someone who had so little respect for me as a human being. I didn't know what he was going to do with me, but I wasn't going to be his whore.

Absolutely not.

I didn't see Crewe much over the next few days. He stayed in his office or worked with Ariel while I stayed outside. When I was underneath the sky, I didn't feel so trapped. The sun warmed my skin just as it did to everyone else, and that made me feel connected to the friends I'd left behind.

When I explored the island and the creatures, I felt invigorated with life again. It made me forget about my current circumstances, that I was living in a prison. When the breeze caressed my skin and the sun warmed my nose, I actually felt a small sense of joy.

The helicopter landed in the field at midday, the propellers spinning until they finally came to a standstill. I eyed the black chopper and wondered if I could figure out how to operate it. If I had access to the internet, I could teach myself in a few months, but Crewe made sure I couldn't access anything.

That bastard.

One of his henchman, Dunbar, approached me at the cliff, wearing black jeans with a gun on his hip.

I didn't trust him. He was unpredictable and impossible to read. I could get a reading on Crewe's emotions, but this guy wore a mask.

He stopped five feet away from me. "Come inside."

"Don't boss me around." I could sit there as long as I liked.

He stepped closer to me then grabbed me by the throat, squeezing me so tight I couldn't breathe. Crewe grabbed my neck dozens of times, but he never tightened his grip like this. His touches always implied warning but didn't carry eminent threat.

I tried to kick Dunbar, but my legs were too short.

Dunbar watched my face turn blue. "If you don't want to suffocate, I suggest you listen to me." He pressed his face closer to mine. "Got it?"

I nodded, desperate for air.

He released me and stood back. "Up"

I clutched my throat and took a deep breath. My throat was irritated, so I heaved on the ground, choking even though his hand wasn't around my throat anymore. Every time I took a breath, I had to cough again.

"I said get up." Dunbar kicked me in the side, hitting me right in the ribs.

I toppled over and clutched my side as I coughed. I didn't cry out in pain, refusing to give him that satisfaction. I couldn't make a sound anyway because I couldn't stop coughing.

When I didn't get up, he lunged for me again.

"Dunbar." The authoritative voice came from behind me, full of command.

Dunbar stepped back, his hands by his sides. "Just trying to get the bitch up."

"I'll handle her." Crewe appeared above me, in a gray suit with a black tie. "Prepare the chopper." He dismissed him with a cold look.

Dunbar knew he had done something wrong because he walked away without another word.

When he was a few feet away, Crewe turned to him. "Dunbar."

He turned around, looking his employer in the eye.

"Don't touch her like that again." Crewe didn't raise his voice, but the threat in his tone was unmistakable.

Even I was a little afraid.

Dunbar nodded. "I apologize, sir. I was only trying—"

"Come to me if she's a problem. You're dismissed."

Dunbar shut his mouth and walked away, following his orders with stiff shoulders.

Crewe kneeled down and examined me, touching the skin on my side. "Your ribs aren't broken. Just bruised."

"Am I supposed to be grateful?" I sat up and massaged my throat.

His fingers moved to my chin, and he gently shifted my head, getting a look at my neck. "You'll be fine."

"I know," I said defensively. "I never said I wouldn't be." Crewe just helped me but I was angry with him. I was angry that I allowed a man to be so ruthless with me to begin with. I should have fought back harder. I should have broken Dunbar's nose the second he touched me. From my position on the ground, it was impossible.

"You remind me of myself sometimes." He pulled his fingertips away, watching me with the same angry expression he gave Dunbar. "We hate showing weakness to anyone."

"I'm not weak…" I massaged my neck and coughed again.

"I never said you were." He rose to his full height and extended his hand. "Now, get up. If you make me ask you again, I'll be worse than Dunbar."

Now I was livid. "You just told him off for hurting me, but you're going to be worse?" That didn't make any sense.

"You're my property," he said quietly. "I'm the only one who can punish you. Just like a child, only the parent should spank him. Now get your ass up, or I'll drag you back to the house by your hair. What's it gonna be?"

I knew Crewe wasn't bluffing this time. He had no problem backhanding me or gripping me by the neck. There were certain lines he wouldn't cross, but there were plenty that he would. I got to my feet and cleared my throat, still feeling the sting from Dunbar's icy grip.

Crewe stepped away, satisfied with my obedience. "Finley will make you some tea."

I crossed my arms over my chest as I walked beside him. "Why do you want me back at the house?"

"We're leaving for Glasgow. I have business to attend to."

I stopped in my tracks. "I'm going with you?"

"Yes."

I was getting off this island. Once we were in Scotland, I could make a run for it. There had to be an embassy or police station that could help me. Even if I were in another country, I was still kidnapped and they were required to help me.

Crewe read the expression in my eyes. "You aren't getting away, Lovely. You can try. But keep this in mind. If you fail, there will be serious consequences." He stared me down with his mocha-colored eyes, the threat heavy in his voice. "I won't tell you what they are. I'll let your imagination do the work."

My arms tightened around my body, a cold shiver running down my spine. Despite the tone in his voice, my mind was still made up. If I didn't run for it when I had the chance, I would regret it for the rest of my life. Even if he beat me bloody, it would still be worth it.

I just had to be smart about it—and run like hell.

Crewe continued walking, his suit framing his muscular body. Now that I'd seen him naked, I knew what was underneath that tailored suit. He was ripped with muscle, a lean and toned frame that my fingernails enjoyed digging into. My feelings for him were so contradictory. I was still attracted to him, got wet for him, but I despised him at the same time.

How was that even possible?

We entered the house, and I spotted the bags by the door.

"I packed enough things for you for a few days," Finley said. "Dunbar will bring you more clothes in Glasgow if you need them."

"Thanks, Finley." He was the only person in this house that made me smile.

"Finley," Crewe said in his authoritative tone. "Make Lady London some tea with lemon, please. She has a sore throat."

"Of course," Finley said. "Milk?"

"Just black," Crewe said, remembering how I take my coffee.

Finley got to work in the kitchen while Dunbar grabbed the bags and carried everything to the black chopper. Crewe's phone rang, so he stepped into the living room to take the call, speaking quietly so no one would overhear him.

Finley handed me a plastic cup with a lid. "Here you are."

"Thank you." I felt the heat through the cup and knew it was too hot to drink.

Finley checked to see that Crewe was still in the other room before he whispered, "Mr. Donoghue is not exactly what he seems. Life hasn't always been on his side."

I stared at Finley and forgot about the tea in my hands. "What does that mean?"

Finley had a guilty look on his face, as if he knew he'd said too much. "He had a hard life, Lady London. He has a lot of vendettas, a lot of bitterness. He tries to convince himself he's just as evil as his enemies…but he never is. He has a lot of compassion that he tries to hide."

"What happened to him—" I fell quiet when Crewe walked back into the room, no longer on the phone. I tried to cover up our conversation so it wouldn't be obvious we were just talking about him. "Thank you for the tea."

"Of course, Lady London." Finley gave a swift bow before he walked away.

Crewe came to my side, displeasure written all over his face. He suddenly grabbed my wrist, his hands squeezing me with authority. He didn't grab me the way Dunbar did, with pure violence. He led me outside toward the chopper. "Don't stick your nose where it doesn't belong." He stopped walking and pulled me harder into his chest. His hand never left my wrist and his face was close enough for a kiss. "Do you understand me?"

I didn't correct him and tell him that Finley mentioned his past first, because I didn't want that sweet old man to face Crewe's wrath. "There's nothing wrong with wanting to know more about the man who stole me."

His hand moved to my neck, and his lips were practically on mine.

A thrill coursed up my spine, my body immediately reacting to him in a carnal way. There was something about his strength, his power, that attracted me. I didn't put up with bullshit, and it was rare to find a man with a spine and a cock made of steel.

"Do you understand me?" He didn't tighten his grip, refusing to truly hurt me. Now that I'd experienced worse men, I realized I really was safer with Crewe than anyone else. At first, I thought his touches were harsh. But in actuality, they were gentle. They were full of lust rather than hatred.

"Yes." I obeyed willingly, not wanting to push his temper. I could handle this version of him, the silently threatening one. If I didn't push him further than necessary, he would never cause me pain.

"Yes, *sir*."

Now that was something I couldn't get on board with. "You're lucky you got a yes out of me. Don't push your luck."

His eyes shifted as he stared into mine. The chopper came to life in the background, the propeller growing loud and the wind picking up. His hand never left my neck as he looked me dead in the eyes. His thumb brushed across my soft skin. Instead of growing angry at my disobedience, he seemed to soften.

He leaned in and closed the distance between us, giving

me a hard kiss on the mouth. His free hand dug into my hair, getting a grip on the strands as his lips pressed against mine.

I didn't pull away—because I liked it.

He wanted me to obey him and grew angry when I didn't, but he seemed to respect me more when I held my ground. Two contradicting traits in a single man. It didn't add up.

The kiss lasted for several seconds, but it seemed like an eternity. Then he pulled away, his soft lips no longer warm against my mouth. He gave me a final look before he gripped me by the hand and pulled me to the helicopter. "Let's go, Lovely."

Glasgow was a large city in the western region, connected to a wide river that stretched out to the coast. Once we landed on the airstrip, I noticed the intricate architecture of all the buildings. They were Victorian and breathtaking. It seemed like I'd walked into the eighteenth century, with automobiles in the background.

Once the helicopter landed, Crewe's men greeted us on the airstrip, all carrying guns in their holsters. In jeans and dark clothing, they looked like an undercover swat team. They escorted us to the back of a tinted town car, and we drove off through the city.

Crewe looked out the window, his knees wide apart as his fingertips rested on his lips. I recalled how it felt to sit in his lap, to straddle those hips and take his impressive cock. He was the biggest I'd ever taken, and when I fucked him, I really did feel like a virgin. I wasn't used to having sex with a man like that.

We passed through the motorways until we exited the center of the city, moving through the greenery and the trees until we approached a gray castle made out of ancient slabs of stone.

I could hardly believe what I was looking at.

"Are we going there?" I asked, feeling dumb for asking the question. There was no other destination that the eye could see. There was nowhere else to go.

He kept his eyes out the window. "Yes."

"Isn't this property government-owned?"

"No."

I stared at the towering piece of history as we came closer, realizing it was ten times the size of the average mansion. The fortifications were indestructible. It stood the test of time for hundreds of years. "Is it yours?"

"Yes."

I knew he was rich, but who the hell could afford to buy a castle? "This place must have cost a fortune."

"It didn't cost me anything. I'm descended from the House of Alpin."

I wasn't going to sugarcoat it. I didn't know shit about world history. "I'm sorry, I don't know what that means…"

"My bloodline comes from royalty. My ancestors used to rule over Scotland. I'm the last living descendant of the house. Therefore, it's mine."

My jaw dropped in shock. I knew there were some royal families in the world, like in England and a few other places, but I never thought I would meet a descendant of royal blood. "Wow… That's unbelievable."

He shrugged like it was only somewhat interesting.

"I don't mean this offensively, but…you don't look Scottish."

"Because I don't have red hair?" he asked with a bored

voice. "Because I don't have freckles and blue eyes? It's called evolution, Lovely. I figured you would know that since you're an aspiring doctor…"

"No need to be an ass," I snapped. "It's one thing to be Scottish and not look Scottish. It's another to be of royal blood and not look the part. Like I said, I didn't mean it offensively."

The car approached the house, pulling up to the impressive roundabout along the entryway. Fields and trees extended in every direction, making it seem like we were the only people in the known world.

"I can't believe how beautiful it is…"

"Wait until you see the inside." The car stopped, and the driver opened the back door for Crewe.

Crewe took my hand and helped me out, his hand moving to my waist once I was on my feet. I stared at the high walls and the walkways outside the castle. I felt like I had stepped back in time, into another world.

I ignored his hand on my waist as I took in the spectacular sight. I'd never seen anything like this in my life, and to witness it with a man descended from this history was even more remarkable. "Did you have to do any work on it?"

"A little. But for the most part, it held up pretty well." Crewe eyed the remaining cars as they pulled into the driveway, the rest of his crew. His hand rested on top of my hips, his fingers around my waist.

"Why are you touching me like that?" I asked, looking up at him.

"So the men understand you aren't available. Unless you want them to think you're a whore up for grabs?" He dropped his hand from my waist and walked to join his men, leaving me behind.

I definitely didn't want them to think that, but I would tell them that on my own—with my fist.

We approached the entrance to the castle, stopping in front of the two large wooden doors that were at least ten feet tall. We entered a historic entryway, showcasing a high-vaulted ceiling with one enormous fireplace against the back wall. The furniture was Victorian, matching the architecture of the castle. Two different staircases went in opposite directions, and the large rug on the floor was deep burgundy with a lion in the center.

"Where are we taking the girl's stuff?" Dunbar asked, holding one of my bags.

"I have a name," I hissed. "London—and you know that."

He gave Crewe a suppressed glare, silently asking for permission to slap me.

"My quarters," Crewe commanded.

"Uh, hold on." I walked up to Crewe so we could have some form of privacy. "I'm not sleeping with you."

"You think I'm gonna let you out of my sight?" Both of his eyebrows furrowed. "I don't think so."

I didn't know what else to say, so I just repeated myself. "I'm not sleeping with you. You don't even want me to sleep with you."

He leaned his face toward mine, his lips just an inch away. "Maybe we won't be sleeping."

His chambers were from another time. The bed was larger than any king I'd ever seen, the fireplace was bigger than a 70-inch flat screen, and the wood of the dressers and furniture seemed to be refurbished, relics from the ancient castle.

While he worked downstairs with his men in one of the drawing rooms, I stayed in the bedroom, which had its own living room, private balcony, walk-in closet, fully-renovated bathroom, and another sitting room (for what, I couldn't tell you). It was bigger than most houses.

I got goose bumps once I sat on the foot of the bed and wrapped my hand around the bed post. Was this the same bed frame that the last king had slept in? What else in this castle had lived more lifetimes than I would ever see? The historical significance shook me to the core, which was saying something because I never cared for history. But I could appreciate something that was two hundred years old.

I got ready for bed and changed into the baggiest shirt and the ugliest sweatpants I could find. All the clothes Crewe had gotten for me were girly and tight, way too sexy. So I put on his clothes instead. Hopefully, that would deter him from trying to seduce me. Even if he was an unofficial monarch of Scotland, rich, and handsome, I wasn't sleeping with him again.

I was lying in bed, fully awake and looking out the window, when he walked inside. He quietly shut the door behind me like I might be asleep then undressed at the foot of the bed, removing his tie as well as the rest of his suit.

It must have been two in the morning, and it baffled me that he worked for so long. What did they talk about down there? How much intelligence could be discussed for so long? I hadn't fallen asleep yet because I wanted to be awake when he returned. I knew I could trust him, to a certain extent, but I would feel more comfortable once he was in bed and asleep—not awake and stirring.

He pulled back the covers and got in beside me. He didn't touch me, staying on his side of the bed. "Can't sleep?"

How did he know I was awake? "I was waiting for you."

The arrogance showed in his voice. "Oh yeah? Well, I'm right here, Lovely." He moved toward my side of the bed.

I turned over and stuck out my arm, hitting him in his hard chest. "That's not what I meant, and you know it."

He chuckled and kept his distance, moving to his back and staring up at the ceiling. One hand rested on his chest.

I wondered if he was nude. Anytime I came into his room at night, he usually was.

"Why are we sleeping together?" I asked. "You kicked me out of your room last time we were in the same bed."

"That was different."

"How?"

"I don't want you to sleep alone in a room here. One of the guys might go in there and try to have some fun with you…"

The meaning of his words made me tense up. "For loyal men, you don't seem to trust them."

"Actually, I do trust them. But it's when you trust someone the most that you need to be careful."

I raised an eyebrow. "That makes absolutely no sense."

"Not really. Think about it. If my men know I trust them, they'll feel comfortable. And if they feel comfortable, they might try to pull something because they think they can get away with it. Then later they can lie about it, since they know they're in my good graces. So, in my opinion, it's best to play it safe. I'd rather have you under my watch. If you want something done right, you should do it yourself. That's what they say, right?"

Oddly enough, that actually did make a lot of sense.

"No, I don't want to share a bed with you. But this mattress is big enough that I'll hardly notice you're there." He turned his head my way, his hair slightly messy from running his fingers through it. "You don't snore, right?"

"No. Do you?"

"No." He faced the ceiling again.

I stared at his muscled chest, seeing the sheets come up to his waist. "You aren't naked under there, right?"

When he turned back to me, he wore an evil grin. "Why don't you take a peek and find out?"

"I'm good," I said sarcastically.

"Well, he's ready whenever you are."

Whenever I'm ready? Like I'm ever going to be ready. "I'm never going to sleep with you again. That was a one-time thing."

"Whatever you say, Lovely."

"I'm serious."

"I'm sorry," he said with a chuckle. "I have a very hard time believing you."

"I'm not one of your bimbos."

"Whoa." He sat up in bed, propping himself on one

elbow. "What makes you think I see bimbos? As a matter of fact, I like strong, clever, and independent women. One of my girls is a French diplomat. She's smart as hell."

"You have multiple girlfriends?" I asked in disgust.

"No girlfriends. Just girls." He laid back down and pulled the sheets to his shoulder. "There you go again…being jealous."

"Oh, geez…" I wanted to smack him upside the head. "I'm not jealous. I've never been jealous. I'll never be jealous."

"You like to talk about my sex life a lot."

"I really don't," I said coldly. "You're clean, right?" I silently hated myself for asking this question after the act had been committed. But I was doing it to survive, to get away from Bones, so I couldn't be too hard on myself.

"Of course, Lovely. By the way, we need to give you the shot. Ariel will take care of it in the morning."

Now I grew angry. "I said I'm not going to sleep with you."

"Fine. But we're giving you the shot anyway—because you'll change your mind."

"Will not—"

He crawled on top of me and pressed his mouth to mine, giving me a scorching kiss that was so aggressive my mouth ached. His hands gripped my wrists and pinned them to the mattress underneath me. His tongue darted into my mouth and danced with mine.

My resistance disappeared once he breathed into my mouth. His eyes were open, giving me a seductive look as he worshipped my mouth with his. He was naked from the waist down, and I felt his cock against my sweatpants.

When he felt my mouth reciprocate, he released my hand and dug his fingers into my hair, feeling the soft strands. He started to rock with me, his cock rubbing against my clitoris through my sweatpants.

My knees automatically fell apart to give him room because I wanted more of that friction, more of that length of steel to make me feel good. His lips hypnotized me, giving me a kiss so scorching it left me breathless. I instantly forgot this man was my captor, taking away all my human rights, the second he kissed me.

He thrust his hips harder, pushing his cock directly onto my throbbing clitoris. He made me pant and rock with him, enjoying how impressive his length was. I moaned into his mouth when I felt the ecstasy between my legs. Without even being inside me, he made me explode like a firework. "Oh god…" My toes curled, and my moans turned into whimpers. It felt so good that I forgot how easily he got me in the mood.

He stopped rocking and looked down at me, victory in his eyes. "You'll get the shot in the morning."

CREWE

It was ten in the morning, but that didn't stop Ariel and me from sharing a bottle of scotch.

"Are you going to Her Highness' ball next Saturday?" She poured another glass and swished the ice cubes around before she took a drink.

I had completely forgotten about that. "If you told her I was attending, then I must."

"I'm sure that fucking slut will be there." Ariel rolled her eyes, her glasses amplifying the movement.

I smiled when Ariel was protective of me. "Couldn't care less if she is there. But I'd like to bring London along. It doesn't hurt to have a gorgeous woman on my arm."

"Well, that's not possible."

"How so?" I looked at the flames in the hearth of the drawing room. The only thing I despised about this castle was its lack of windows. It was built at a time when fortification was important. When I renovated it, I kept everything exactly the same wherever possible, so I refused to add windows just for the sake of it.

"You really think London will behave herself in front of a majority of the world's royal families?" she asked incredulously. "That woman can't be controlled even with a leash around her throat. You'd have to be out of your mind to take her along."

She was definitely a loose cannon.

"And as far as I can tell, there's nothing to keep her in line. She's not afraid of you."

"That's not entirely true." There were some things I wouldn't do and some things I would.

"Whether it is or isn't doesn't matter." She drank her scotch quicker than I did, able to hold her liquor just the way I could. "You should go alone. It's always easier that way."

I still wanted her on my arm. London's charms had grown

on me. She had a beautiful smile on the rare occasions she showed it, and her body was nothing but curves. In a gown with styled hair and makeup, she would outshine everyone in the room. "I still want to take her."

Ariel didn't hide her look of annoyance. "Why are men always so stupid when it comes to women? Time and time again. Just remember Helen of Troy before you do anything stupid."

"I have an idea of how to keep her in line."

She set her glass down and crossed her arms over her chest. "Really? Let's hear this idea."

I poured another glass before I gave her the name that would explain everything else. "Joseph Ingram."

After a moment of consideration, she smiled. "Not a bad idea."

Ariel followed me into the royal chambers with the proper equipment. London was in the second living room next to the balcony, reading a book she found on the shelf.

"Ariel is going to give you the shot," I announced as we walked inside.

London nearly jumped out of her skin at my unannounced presence. "Geez, a heads-up would have been nice…"

"Don't forget you're beneath us," Ariel said coldly. "Drop the entitlement, and shut your mouth."

London's eyes snapped open, affronted by the cold insult.

I tried not to smile. Ariel was a lot to take in—until you got to know her.

"You're a disgrace to women, you know that?" London stood up like she was prepared to fight her. "He's keeping me as a prisoner against my will and you stand by and do nothing. He's stripped me of my clothes—"

"If you're done whining, I have work to do." Ariel opened her briefcase on the wooden table.

London's jaw dropped, shocked that Ariel could be so foul. She turned to me in shock. "This woman is your business partner? Does she talk to everyone like this?"

"Just the ones who annoy me." Ariel tested the syringe before she sat on the couch. "Don't expect me to feel sorry for you just because I'm a woman. If you don't like your circumstance, change it. It's that simple."

"You think I want to be here?" London asked incredulously.

Ariel pointed to the cushion beside her, silently commanding her to take a seat. "I think you need birth control because you enjoy fucking the man who captured you. So yes, I do think you want to be here."

London glanced at the vase sitting on the nearby table.

I knew exactly what she was going to do next. "Don't even think about it, Lovely." I grabbed her by the wrist before she could do anything that could get her killed. I guided her to the seat and sat beside her, keeping an eye on both of them.

London was so angry she couldn't speak—which was a first.

Ariel inserted the needle and deposited the fluid. Then it was over. She placed a cotton ball against the skin and covered it with a bandage. "You'll be ready to go in twenty-four hours." She put her supplies away then walked out, leaving us alone together.

I knew London was eager to speak her mind.

"That woman is horrible."

I shrugged. "She's not that bad when she likes you."

"Does she insult all of your clients like that?"

When I thought about it, I smiled. "Actually, yeah."

"And that's okay?" she asked incredulously.

Ariel had a lot of valuable qualities that couldn't be replaced. "She's the best at what she does. That's all I can say."

"And what is that, exactly?"

I never told her about my other company. "She pretty much runs my scotch business. I just oversee a few things here and there."

"Wait…you make scotch?" she asked in surprise. The realization slowly dawned on her, probably thinking about all the times she caught me drinking the amber liquid throughout the day. "I guess it makes sense."

"It's my clean money, how I launder all my other cash."

She nodded like she understood. "And she works with your intelligence stuff too?"

"Yeah. She does a lot."

London sighed when she realized there was no way to get rid of her nemesis. "I haven't done anything to earn her hatred. She's pretty cruel."

"It's nothing personal. She doesn't like people she doesn't know."

"Well, she didn't know everyone at one point."

"And honestly, she still doesn't like me now."

London actually chuckled. "Can't blame her…"

I liked seeing her smile—for me. It was an expression she hardly wore, like a rain cloud in the desert. "Give it time. She'll come around." I examined the cotton ball stuck to her arm, knowing within twenty-four hours I could have her the way I wanted. "Looks like you're ready to go."

Her smile dropped instantly.

I knew she was at war with herself. Her body craved mine, especially after the exquisite orgasms I gave her. But her mind couldn't accept the attraction, not under the inhumane circumstance. She would always see me as the man who imprisoned her, a dictator.

But that was all about to change soon enough.

13

LONDON

He came to bed late that night again, finishing up work downstairs with Ariel and the rest of his crew. I didn't bother to pretend to be asleep this time. He walked inside and undid his tie, his eyes finding mine. Seductively, he removed every single item of clothing and dropped them on the floor. First, it was the tie and then it was the collared shirt. He undid his belt and bent it in his hands, testing the tightness. Then he dropped his slacks.

I eyed his near-naked body and felt repulsed by my immediate arousal. For a criminal, he had soft and flawless skin. The muscles coiled and moved every time he shifted, his power obvious in his build. He wasn't bulky like Dunbar, but his long and lean look implied he was strong—but also fast.

He kicked off his shoes and socks then grabbed the brim of his boxers next.

I knew I shouldn't look. I wasn't sure why I was looking in the first place.

His brown eyes held a vibrant desire and confidence that was borderline arrogant. He pulled them down his waist until his hard cock appeared, the head swollen and a darker shade than the rest of his length. Nine inches of man emerged from his trimmed balls. He kicked the boxers aside then came to the bed, knowing he had my full attention.

He got into bed beside me and rested one arm underneath his head. The sheets bunched up to his waist, only the outline of his hard cock noticeable. Without trying, he looked like every woman's dream. Masculine, powerful, and sexy. He was sleeping inside a castle that was passed on to him through his noble blood. He really was a king.

He turned his head and looked at me, his five o'clock shadow thicker than it was that morning. "Like what you see, Lovely?"

I didn't bother lying anymore. It was obvious how attracted I was to him. But no matter how strong my needs were, I wasn't going to go down that road. I had too much respect for myself, and my desire for freedom had never faltered. I couldn't succumb to something so carnal and forget what was important. I may not be able to stop him from seducing me, but I could make sure I wasn't making the first move. "I'm tired…" I yawned and turned over, trying to forget about the aching throb between my legs.

He turned off the bedside lamp and chuckled. "Whatever you say, Lovely. But very soon, you'll be giving me exactly what I want."

My heart quickened at his words. "What's that supposed to mean?"

"You'll see in the morning." He fell silent, refusing to give up any more information.

I didn't take his threats lightly. He had power, money, and authority. He could make a lot of things happen—anything. I didn't know what he was going to pull in the morning, but I had to make sure I wasn't around to find out.

I concentrated on his breathing, studying it to determine what stage he was in during his REM cycle. I couldn't make my move unless he was out cold. I was in the middle of nowhere, and I needed as much of a head start as possible.

When his breathing turned deep and constant, I slipped out of bed and put on the running shoes Dunbar had placed in my bag. I was in black leggings and a t-shirt, poor clothes for a quick getaway, but they would have to do.

I crept to the door on the other side of the room and slowly opened it, grateful it didn't creak due to its old age. I stepped into the hallway and looked left and right, making sure no one was on guard. The deep red rug stretched down the hallway, underneath the crystal chandeliers which hung from the ceiling.

I crept down the hallway and stuck close to the wall, listening for any sound. I reached the end and peered down the stairway, seeing no one at the bottom. I crept down to the bottom floor, and my eyes immediately darted to the two enormous doors that marked the entryway.

Dunbar stood in front of them, dressed in all black. He looked at his phone like he might be playing a game to pass the time.

Damn. I couldn't go that way.

I went back upstairs and took the hallway on the opposite side of the room, which went down a corridor of bedrooms. One room I passed had a woman moaning loudly while the bed creaked, and I couldn't help but think of Crewe and what we could be doing right now if I hadn't left.

Shake it off.

I had to get the hell out of there.

I took different hallways left and right, eventually getting lost in the enormous castle. The amount of power used to keep the lights on must be exorbitant. I moved to the opposite end and peered through the large window that overlooked the castle. From what I could gauge, I was on the opposite side of the property now, above a courtyard with rose bushes inside a garden.

The only staircases led back to the main entryways, and I had to assume they were all blocked. I had years of mountain climbing experience, so I could climb down to the bottom. I was on the third floor, so it was dangerous.

But it was worth the risk.

None of the windows opened, so I walked to a bedroom

in the corner. Careful not to make a sound, I crept inside, relieved to see no one was occupying it. And to my luck, it had a balcony. I shut the door and locked it behind me.

The balcony was on top of the third roof. The only way I could get down was if I crawled along the grooves of the stones. It was dangerous and borderline stupid. There was grass at the bottom instead of concrete, but it was still so far of a fall that I would probably break something.

In the back of my mind, I heard Crewe's warning. If I tried to escape and failed, there would be serious consequences. I knew the threat was sincere, and I would seriously pay for my actions. I could chicken out and return to the bedroom. Or I could continue forward and hope for the best.

I had to get out of here.

I threw my legs over the edge and slowly began to descend, digging my nails into the grooves over the stones to hold my weight up. Within a minute, my skin began to burn at the contact. The exertion caused me to sweat. I gritted my teeth as I moved down, refusing to look at the ground and risk losing my footing.

I was halfway to the bottom when I heard the shouts.

"Find her!" Crewe's terrifying voice echoed across the

courtyard, reaching my ears even though he was clear on the other side of the property.

Shit.

I glanced down and knew I still had a way to go, but I didn't have time to take it slow. I had to jump and hope for the best. After I took a deep breath, I let go.

I landed on the grass and rolled, coming out of my fall without any broken bones. My joints ached at the momentum my body felt against the earth, but that was nothing compared to how bad it could have been.

Flashlights erupted throughout the castle, in windows and on balconies, followed by irritated voices.

I had to get out of there.

I sprinted through the courtyard and headed for the trees, my heart beating so fast it threatened to burst. My feet struck the earth loudly, but I kept going, needing to break the tree line. Once I was in the wild with the trees and meadows, I could hide until they finally gave up. They may be patient, but I was determined.

"There's that little bitch!" Dunbar flashed his light on my shoulder, catching me in my sprint.

Fuck. Fuck. Fuck.

I shifted my body into gear and ran as hard as I could. Being cooped up on Fair Isle hindered my stamina. I was in pretty good shape before I left New York, on my feet all day at the hospital. But my fitness level had taken a serious hit.

That didn't stop me.

"Here!" Dunbar's voice was terrifying because it was so loud. He was close by, just yards behind me.

I wasn't going to make it.

But I couldn't give up just yet. I would never give up.

I broke through the tree line and kept running, finally reaching the highlands. It was dark in the wilderness, the moonlight not enough to direct me. But even if I had a flashlight, I couldn't use it.

I knew I couldn't outrun Dunbar. He was in too good of shape.

I had to hide.

I sprinted past a tall tree and dug my feet into the earth as I stopped. Without thinking twice about it, I ran up the trunk and grabbed a thick branch. I hoisted myself up, ignoring the splinters of wood that impaled my palms, and kept going. I climbed as far as I could before the branches thinned out and couldn't hold my weight.

Then I sat there, trying not to breathe loudly. These guys weren't just average men. They worked for Crewe, so they were worth their salt. It shouldn't be hard to figure out where I was.

But I could get lucky.

Dunbar's voice was far too close for my liking. "She's hiding. Probably in one of these trees."

Goddammit.

Lights flashed everywhere as a dozen men walked around my location, shining their flashlights up neighboring trees and bushes. Dunbar's heavy boots crunched against the grass as he came close to my hiding place.

Blood pounded in my ears as I gripped the tree branch I was perched on. I wasn't going to get away, and I would have to suffer Crewe's cruel punishment. My imagination ran wild and utterly terrified me.

Dunbar walked to the bottom of the tree, right in my line of sight. I could see his thick silhouette with his flashlight pointed to the ground. Then he turned and pointed the light upward right at me.

His smile could be heard in his voice. "Gotcha."

All the hope drained from my body. I felt defeated, even stupid.

Dunbar shoved his fingers into his mouth and gave a loud whistle. "She's over here, boys."

There was nowhere for me to go.

His Scottish accent carried his condescending tone. "I'll climb up there and drag you down if I have to. But we both know it would be easier if you came down here on your own. There's nowhere to run or hide. And the boss will be here any second."

Tears sprang to my eyes but didn't fall. All I craved was freedom, to be respected as a human being again. I missed walking to the coffee shop around the corner from my house, standing under the sunlight without fear of someone taking my rights away.

"What's it gonna be?" he asked angrily.

There was no other plan for escape. Instead of drawing it out, I climbed down. I moved from branch to branch and slowly got to the ground. I released the last branch I was holding and my shoes hit the grass.

Dunbar immediately grabbed me by the neck and threw me hard onto the ground. "Stay there."

I obeyed without giving attitude. The men surrounded me with their flashlights, their silhouettes obvious. Sometimes I caught a glimpse of their faces from a neighboring flashlight. When the crowd parted, I knew they were making way for their leader.

Their king.

He slowly approached me on the ground and loomed over me, his black silhouette ominous. His anger was palpable, terrifying. He radiated fierce authority, turning into the dictator he truly was.

He kneeled in front of me, his face visible from the lights of the circle. His brown eyes were cruel, no longer charming. He didn't say a single word but he didn't need to. His stare was intimidating enough.

"What. Did. I. Say." His voice came out as a whisper, full of threat. His hand shot out and he gripped me by the neck, squeezing me harder than he ever had before. He constricted my throat until I couldn't breathe.

The sad thing was, I didn't blame him for hurting me. He gave me a fair warning. I took the risk anyway when I didn't have a solid plan. I should have scouted the area more, learned the layout of the castle. But when the following day loomed over my head, I panicked.

He squeezed me tighter, cutting off my airway altogether. "Get. Your. Ass. Up." He stood and dragged me with him, forcing me to my feet without the gentleness he always used to handle me with. He pushed me aside. "Walk."

I walked forward, feeling him behind me. I led the way, knowing a dozen men followed me, all their flashlights pointed at my back. I felt like livestock about to be slaughtered. My feet moved slowly, procrastinating as much as possible.

I felt Crewe's eyes drill into my back.

Like a criminal walking to his own grave, I felt like this was the end.

We returned to the castle entryway. I didn't know where he wanted me to go next, so I stood there, still tall but no longer proud.

"I'll take it from here." Crewe's hand returned to my neck, and he guided me upstairs, walking me like a dog with his arm as a leash. Even though I'd been nothing but cooperative, he still nearly strangled me.

We arrived at the royal chamber, and he shoved me inside. "Strip."

Oh god.

He slammed the door and stood behind me, his heavy breaths falling on my neck. "Don't make me ask you again."

I knew I wouldn't be able to talk my way out of this one. I kept my eyes straight ahead as I pulled my shirt over my head and tossed it aside.

Crewe leaned against the foot of the bed and crossed his arms over his chest. He stared me down coldly, his brown eyes not possessing even a hint of compassion.

I unclasped my bra and let it fall, trying not to feel so defeated. This man had seen me naked before, and fucked me on his bed and made me come. I shouldn't feel embarrassed or weak. I felt a lot more comfortable now than I did the first time he commanded me to undress.

He watched me with angry eyes, not showing any arousal.

I kicked off my shoes and pulled down my leggings, taking my underwear with them. Then I stood naked in front of him, unsure what would happen next. I hoped he would take me from behind on the bed. Since the sex was good, that didn't sound so bad. But that wouldn't be much of a punishment.

The slacks he wore earlier were back on, along with his collared shirt. Even in the middle of the night, he refused to let his men see him at anything less than his best. He pulled his belt out of the loops of his pants then bent it in half. He pulled on the ends and made it snap together, causing a loud clap. "I'm going to punish you for what you've done. I'm going to spank you ten times and turn your ass red in reparations. So climb on the bed, ass in the air."

He was going to spank me like a child? "That's it?"

He made the belt snap again. "Don't worry, Lovely. It'll hurt. And I'll enjoy hurting you."

I couldn't remember if I'd ever been spanked.

"Ass in the air," he said with authority. "Now."

I moved around him and crawled on the bed. My feet hung over the edge, and I pressed my cheek to the sheets. My ass was raised toward the ceiling, at the perfect position for him to whip me.

He came behind me and ran the leather gently over the

skin, feeling the smoothness between both objects. Then he ran his hands over one cheek, giving it a tight squeeze. "You really pissed me off tonight, Lovely. I've been more lenient than I should be. But now that's over."

I gripped the sheets on either side of me, wanting this to end as quickly as possible.

He shifted behind me, his knees moving to the stone floor. His warmth breaths blew on my entrance, and I wondered what would happen next. Just when I turned to look, I felt his warm mouth kiss my most vulnerable area.

Oh wow…

His tongue worked my clit before he sucked it into his mouth.

I'd never had a man do that to me before, and as terrified as I was, it still felt incredible.

He gripped my thighs as his tongue delved inside me, tasting and exploring me. He worked my clit again, bringing me to the edge of a powerful orgasm. I could feel it approaching over the horizon. He kissed me harder, just as aggressive as when he kissed my mouth.

I was almost there, moaning at his touch. My hands

scooted down the bed until they wrapped around his wrists.

He pushed me further, right on the precipice of euphoria.

Then he pulled away.

No.

He stood up again and grabbed his belt. "Your pussy is just as lovely." He rested the belt on my ass before he pulled it off again. "We're going to count to ten. When I say the number, you repeat it back to me. If you fail to do so, you'll get another. Do you understand me?"

"Yes."

"Yes, *sir*."

I couldn't call him that. This was the most he would get out of me.

When I didn't give him what he wanted, he continued on. "An extra five slaps, it is." He positioned himself behind me before he threw all his weight into the swing of the belt. He hit me so hard I cried out, hearing the slap thud against my ears. He breathed heavily as if he was overexerting himself. But it was just his arousal breaking through the surface. His desire came out, loud and unmistakable. "One."

That was only one?

I didn't want to add another five to the list, so I counted with him. "One…"

He whipped my ass five more times, successfully slapping me in consecutive strokes. He hit the same area over and over, making me cry out in pain. It was a burning sensation I'd never experienced. He didn't go easy on me, striking me as hard as he could. Tears prickled my eyes as the skin began to turn raw.

When we got to ten, he slowed down. "Do you see what happens when you fuck with me?"

I cried quietly into the sheets.

He came around the bed and grabbed me by the hair. He looked into my tear-stained face, showing no compassion. "I warned you, Lovely. I told you not to do it, but you did it anyway. You're never going to learn unless I punish you."

I steadied my tears and met his gaze, trying to find strength somewhere.

"You know you deserve this," he whispered. "Are you going to run away again?"

"No…" I'd never be able to escape, not when a dozen

men accompanied him wherever he went.

"Promise me."

"I promise…" I just wanted it to stop. It wasn't just the pain that bothered me. It was the humiliation of being whipped like a child. It was the fact that I had to lie there and take it. And worst of all, it was the fact that, deep down inside, a part of me liked it. I liked the way he pushed me on the bed and whipped me with dominance. I liked the way he controlled me, controlled the entire world around me. And I wanted him to keep doing what he was doing before with his mouth against my tender skin.

His hand softened and moved through my hair, taking on a gentler touch. "I want to stop, Lovely. But I can't. I have to finish."

"I said I won't do it again…"

"I know." He kissed the corner of my eye like he was truly sorry. "But I'm a man of my word. I can't go back on my punishment."

"You didn't give me to Bones…"

"That was because I had a better use for you. It had nothing to do with sparing you."

This man was more dangerous than I gave him credit for. The only thing he wouldn't do was take me against my will. Everything else was on the table. "Then get it over with."

He kissed me again, his lips moving to the corner of my mouth. "You have no idea how much I want you right now. You have no idea how beautiful you look, your ass in the air and tears on your cheeks. I've never been more aroused in my life than I am in this moment." Somehow, he made the sinister confession actually sound sweet.

He left my side and returned to my rear. He snapped the belt together before he struck me, hitting me just as hard as before. "Eleven."

I winced under the pain. "Eleven…"

He hit me again. "Twelve." His breathing sped up again, his desire to fuck me filling the air between us.

"Twelve…"

"Louder, Lovely."

I deepened my voice. "Twelve."

He slapped the belt across both of my cheeks, hitting at the perfect angle to maximize the pain. "Thirteen."

"Thirteen…"

He threw his entire body into the next one, hitting me so hard I rocked forward. He breathed hard without counting, catching his breath as he stared at my red ass. "Fourteen."

"Fourteen…"

"Last one, Lovely. Let's make it count."

I closed my eyes and waited for it to be over.

He gave me the hardest slap he ever had, making the leather bite into my skin. "Fifteen."

The number tumbled out of my mouth quickly, wanting to make sure he didn't have an excuse to strike me again. "Fifteen."

He dropped the belt on the floor then moved to his knees again. His lips kissed the raw skin of my ass then moved back to the place between my legs. He unzipped his slacks then spit on his hand. "Your pussy is amazing…" He jerked himself off as he sucked my pussy, doing amazing things to my clitoris that made me convulse. The previous pain and the current pleasure lit my body on fire. One hand reached behind me and grabbed his, listening to the sound of his wet hand stroking his cock.

He moaned into my pussy when he was on the verge of coming, his orgasm happening in record time.

Knowing he was about to come made me explode. His lips against my clitoris made my back arch and my jaw unhinge. I released a scream louder than all the rest, sounding like a dying animal. "God…"

He groaned as his mouth remained pressed to my opening, coming with me at the exact same time. "Fuck…"

I enjoyed the high as it swept me away. Slowly, it began to fade. It was the most powerful sensation I'd ever felt, making me writhe and twist. I lost my breath and forgot about the pain coming from my rear. I gave into the dark sensation, thoroughly enjoying it.

Crewe remained on his knees as he recovered from the high. He got to his feet then wiped himself off before he grabbed a jar of ointment. He dipped his fingers inside then spread it across my cheeks, curing the burn almost instantly. "I think we understand each other better now. Don't cross me again."

I learned my lesson.

"Or it'll be thirty slaps."

14

LONDON

When I woke up the following morning, my ass still hurt.

The cheeks were red and irritated, raw from the bite of his leather belt. The cream he put over the welts soothed the pain, but I knew the marks were there without even checking. I opened my eyes and turned over, expecting to see him beside me.

But he wasn't there.

Sometimes he was up early, exercising before he showered and joined his crew downstairs. His schedule was never concrete, so I didn't have a clue what he was doing. It's not like he would tell me if I asked.

I kicked the covers aside then looked out the window,

seeing the morning sunlight sprinkle across the castle. The place looked like a fairytale—even though it didn't feel like one.

As if he knew I was awake, he walked through the door. "Good. You're awake."

"I hope that means you brought breakfast."

He didn't chuckle like he usually would, telling me he was in a particularly bad mood despite the action we got last night. I didn't bother being embarrassed by it. I liked the things he did to me. It was stupid to keep fighting it— and lying about it. "Get dressed and come downstairs. You can have breakfast afterward."

"Is this about that surprise you told me about?"

"Yes." He grabbed a pair of jeans and a t-shirt hanging in the closet and threw them on the bed. "But you probably aren't going to want breakfast afterward."

That didn't sound good.

He approached the bed and grabbed my chin, directing my look toward him even though he already had my full attention. "Fifteen minutes. If you aren't in the drawing room by then, I'll drag you myself—by the hair." He released me, a fiery look still in his eyes.

I wanted to run away again. Whatever was waiting for me downstairs was probably cruel.

"Alright?"

"Yes," I answered immediately, hating myself for doing it.

"Yes, *sir*." He had commanded me to address him that way countless times, but I couldn't do it.

And I still couldn't do it. I couldn't bow to any man. I couldn't kneel. I couldn't surrender, not like that. He may backhand me or worse, but I still couldn't bend to his will. It was an innate part of me, to be defiant whenever possible. He needed control, but I needed it too. We were two sides of the same coin. "I said yes."

His brown eyes narrowed in irritation, but he didn't threaten me with a punishment. Suddenly, a smile crept into his lips, sinister and terrifying. He stepped away and placed his hands in his pockets, somehow pleased by the exchange.

What was I missing?

He walked out, the cruel smile still on his lips. "Fifteen minutes, Lovely."

After I got dressed, I walked downstairs and entered the drawing room with hesitance. I wasn't sure what I was going to find there, but whatever it was, I couldn't avoid it. I stepped inside and saw some of the men standing with their backs to the fire in the hearth, enjoying a drink and each other's company. The others were spread around the room, smoking cigars and drinking scotch. I spotted Crewe in the center, sitting in an oversized red armchair that was made for a king.

Ariel leaned over a man on the floor, dabbing a towel against his neck.

That's when I noticed the pool of blood on the hardwood floor—and the man who was bleeding.

"Joey?" I stifled a cry as I ran to his side, recognizing my brother immediately. His hair was much longer than the last time I saw him, and he looked pale like he hadn't seen the light of day in weeks. "What are you doing to him?"

Ariel held a knife and stitches, obviously finished doing something to him.

Ariel ignored my question like it wasn't important enough to answer.

Instantly, I snapped. I grabbed her by the wrist and yanked her down to the floor. Then I crawled on top of her and slammed my fist into her face. "Don't touch my brother!" I raised my fist to hit her again when I was dragged off her body.

To my annoyance, Crewe kneeled in front of her and examined her face with concern. "Are you alright?" He noticed her bloody lip and pulled out a handkerchief. He kept his voice low, their interaction quiet.

Now I really hated Crewe.

"I'm fine." Ariel pushed him off and got to her feet. "That cunt punches like a girl anyway."

"Oh yeah?" I yanked myself free from the men. "Then let's give it another go."

Crewe raised his hand to silence me. "Enough."

I returned to my knees on the floor and cupped Joey's face. "Joe, it's me." I patted his chest gently, trying to get his attention.

He was in a confused daze, like he had just woken up from anesthesia. "London…?"

"Yes, it's me," I said with relief. "Are you okay?"

"I…" He tried to sit up but appeared too weak.

Crewe's feet appeared on the other side of his body, his shoes shiny and his slacks crisp. "He's out of it right now. Gave him a quick operation."

"What kind of operation?" I looked up, the hatred pounding in my ears.

He pulled out a small black device before he kneeled down so we were at eye level. "Joseph tried to pull another stunt against me. I warned him not to do it, but just like his sister, he never listens. So I have to punish him too."

"Maybe if you stopped trying to control everyone, this wouldn't happen," I hissed.

Crewe ignored the comment. "I'm merciful, so I wanted to give you the opportunity to say goodbye. I've inserted an EMP through his skull and at the underside of his brain. Once I hit this button, he'll have an aneurism and die."

My hands began to shake when I realized I was just seconds away from losing my brother. "I'll give you the money, alright?" My hand automatically grabbed Joey's chest. "Just leave him alone."

"It's not about the money." Crewe played with the remote in his hand, gliding his fingers along the smooth box. "And you know it."

"Just…please." I didn't know what else to say. I couldn't reason with this man. He was too cruel, too evil.

"Don't worry," he said. "I'm not going to pull the trigger. Joseph is going to do it."

"What?"

"Yes. Because if he doesn't kill himself…" Crewe reached behind his back and pulled out a loaded pistol. He cocked the gun before he pointed the barrel right between my eyes. "I'm going to kill you. So he has to choose. You or him."

I'd completely underestimated this man. He was psychotic, insane. "You can't do this…"

"I can, and I will." He nudged Joseph hard in the side. "Did you hear that? You need to choose."

"He's totally out of it," I snapped. "He can't make a decision like this."

"Well, he'll have to." Crewe looked down at my brother. "Now choose."

Joseph opened his eyes and stared at the gun pointed right at my face. Then he glanced at the tracker.

I already knew who he was going to choose.

"What will it be?" Crewe pressed. "You or your sister?"

Joseph raised a shaky hand. "Give it to me…" He cleared his throat and tried to sit up, wanting to appear strong.

Crewe smiled before he handed the tracker over. "Just press the top button, and it'll be over instantly." He turned back to me, the gun still pointed at my face. "Watching your brother end his own life should be punishment enough for both of you."

I turned red in the face because I was so angry. I let this man touch me, kiss me, and he was worse than the devil himself. Every day was worse than the previous one, and now I was going to lose the only family I had left in the world. "Crewe, please. I'll do anything."

"There's nothing you can offer me," he said coldly, holding the gun steady. "Hit the button already, Joseph. The rest of us have lives to live."

"No." I grabbed Joseph's wrist and forced his hand down.

"Crewe, there has to be something you want. I'll give you anything in the world. Just don't do this. Let my brother go. You've gotten enough revenge."

"The only thing I want is something you've proven you can't give." He pressed the barrel against the skin between my eyes.

I didn't have a clue what he was talking about. "What?"

"Obedience. Absolute obedience."

That was something I could never give to anyone—until now. "You want me to obey you? If I do what you ask, you'll let him live?" If that was the case, he was asking for a lot. My body and mind would no longer be my own. Like a dog, I'd have to bark at his command.

"The only way I'd let this asshole go is if you agree to give me your absolute devotion. When I tell you to do something, you do it. No questions asked. You're my slave, my property. Your purpose is to listen to me, to hang on to every single word I say. When I ask you to sit, you sit. When I ask you to suck my cock, you do it and enjoy it. It's a price too high for you to pay. I know you, London. You couldn't handle it."

No, I couldn't. But I would make it happen to save my last family member. "I'll do it, Crewe. Whatever you want." I would let him break me, let him control me exactly the way he wanted. If he wanted to fuck me, he could fuck me.

Crewe finally lowered the gun, cocking his head to the side. "I don't think you understand, London. I'll still have this tracker. The second you fail to please me, I'll hit that button. I'll ask you to do stuff you despise—and act like you enjoy it. I've allowed you to get away with a lot since you came into my possession, but all those freedoms will be gone. Everything will be different."

I did understand the cruelty he implied. I understood I would have to close off my mind and obey his every command. Listening to someone boss me around went against everything I believed in. But I had to do the right thing for my brother. I had to spare him. Eventually, he would figure out how to rescue me. And when he did, I would be free. This imprisonment was only temporary. I could do this.

Crewe continued to watch me with his mocha-colored eyes, the gun still raised. "Are you sure you can handle that?"

I nodded. "Just let him go."

He finally lowered the gun. "Your spine is even harder

than I realized." He stood up and motioned to his men. "Get him out of here."

The men moved to Joseph and gripped him by the arms. His body was limp because he was still out of it, unable to think or speak.

"Where are you taking him?" I demanded.

"Somewhere safe." Crewe shoved the gun into the back of his slacks.

They carried Joseph's body out of the drawing room and to the entryway. I was still terrified for his safety, unsure if he would really be okay. "How do I know you aren't just going to kill him anyway?"

Crewe walked up to me, his face pressed close to mine. His hand moved to my cheek, his thumb brushing across the skin. He was tender with me despite being so inhumane just a moment ago. "I'm a man of my word, Lovely. If I say he's safe, he's safe."

For some idiotic reason, I believed him. "Where?"

"They'll drop him off in a hotel. When he wakes up, he can call his men."

I closed my eyes in relief, needing to know my brother would be okay. I hadn't seen him as often as I would've liked over the past few years, but we were still close. Once our parents died, we stopped being bickering siblings and turned into our own family. He was the one person I would do anything for without hesitation.

"For this plan to work, I need him alive." Crewe continued to reassure me even though I didn't voice my doubts. "I want him to know you're my prisoner, sacrificing yourself so he may live. Everyone will fear me even more than they already do."

That's all he seemed to care about. Money was irrelevant. What he craved was absolute power.

He dropped his hand from my cheek, and his gaze turned cold. His emotions shifted dramatically, from one extreme to the next. His breathing picked up just the way it did when he whipped my ass until it was red. "Go to my quarters, dress yourself up, and take a knee on the hardwood floor. Wait for me."

He issued his first command, and I had to obey. If I didn't, all he had to do was hit the small button, and my brother would be dead. My spine shivered in rebuttal, but I kept my mouth shut. He watched me intently, waiting to see my response. I despised myself for cooperating, but I had to do it. I had to give this king what he wanted. "Yes."

His hand moved to my neck, his fingers wrapping around my throat gently. He pressed his face close to mine, his lips just inches away. He stared at my mouth. "Yes, *sir*."

Revulsion swept through me like a storm. My body internally writhed and burned in anguish. I had to submit to him, to give up my self-respect and perseverance. Despite the circumstance, I still judged myself for cooperating. I refused to let a man boss me around, but now I had to drop my principles—to survive. "Yes…sir."

15

CREWE

I couldn't stop shaking.

I stood outside the royal chambers and stared at my hands. They wouldn't remain still. The second she called me sir, exquisite pleasure crept down my spine all the way to my balls. I almost grabbed her by the hair and pushed her to her knees.

I won.

I finally got her where I wanted her to be, on her knees. A part of me loved her independence and fire, the fact that she refused to be controlled by anyone—especially me. But I also craved her submission. It brought the desire from deep within my bones. I hadn't been this hard since the last time I fucked her.

Now I really wanted to fuck her.

I stood outside the door until I could control my breathing. It was haywire, full of intense desire. I couldn't wait to do so many things to her. Even though she was here against her will, I knew she enjoyed everything I did to her. She enjoyed the kisses, the spanks, and the sex. But she was far too proud to admit it to herself. Her stubbornness was too powerful for her to ignore.

But now she had to.

I opened the door and spotted her on her knees near the bed—exactly where I wanted her. I took another deep breath and shut the door behind me, feeling the heat sear my skin so deeply that it burned. My hard cock pressed against my slacks, eager to break free.

Her hands rested on her lap, and she wore a black dress, something she must have found in the closet. Black heels were on her feet, and her hair was done in lustrous curls. Her makeup was heavy and amplified the natural beauty of her eyes.

She was gorgeous.

I poured myself a glass of scotch and took a seat in the armchair. I stared at her, feeling victorious like a king who'd just conquered a city. I placed the glass against my lips and swallowed the cool liquid, looking at my prize on the floor.

She stared at me without an expression, waiting for further instruction.

I let the victory linger, enjoying the sight of her on her knees on the floor. The position was uncomfortable for her legs as well as her back, but she remained that way out of obedience. I conquered this woman completely and utterly—finally. I wanted to savor the moment as much as possible. "Lovely?"

She locked her eyes on mine and cleared her throat. "Yes, sir?"

Fuck.

I was gonna come just from listening to her.

I took another drink of my scotch to edge myself, feeling my cock twitch inside my pants.

After I let the amber liquid move to my stomach, I set the glass on the armrest. "Up."

She did as I asked, rising to her feet and standing in the black heels. The dress hugged her features perfectly, showing her hourglass shape. Her cleavage was noticeable in the front, and her long legs stretched on for days. "Strip—slowly." With one hand, I undid my tie and let the pieces of silk drape down my chest. "Leave the heels on."

A moment of hesitation flashed in her eyes, but the look was sexy. Every time she struggled, it just reminded me how much she had to force herself to behave. She moved her hands behind her back and undid the zipper slowly, dropping her gaze.

"Eyes on me, Lovely."

She looked at me, her fingers pulling the zipper to the very bottom. The fabric around her shoulders came loose and sunk down her petite frame, revealing a black lace bra against her pale skin.

She pulled the dress over her hips and down her legs, letting it fall to her ankles. She kicked the fabric aside, left only in her heels and underwear.

Fuck, she was gorgeous.

I brought the glass to my lips again even though I wasn't thirsty.

She stepped closer to me, her heels echoing against the hardwood as she came forward. She undid the clasp of her bra and let the strap come loose. It slowly inched down her body until she tossed it aside.

Her tits were beautiful—like always.

I stared at their firmness and roundness. They were slightly big in proportion to her size—and so goddamn perky. I remembered the way her nipples felt in my mouth, absolutely exquisite.

She moved to the black thong next, fingering the lace before she pulled it over her hips and ass and down her legs. She pulled it to her ankles and kicked it away, raising one heel when a piece of the lace got stuck to it.

She was all woman—and all curves. I stared at her navel and then the nub between her legs, appreciating the lack of hair from her perfectly manicured pussy. Her wide hips led to a slender waistline, and then to those gorgeous, eye-popping tits. I could see the hollow of her throat, a piece of her body that would be infected by my kisses soon enough.

"Play with your tits." My voice grew darker the longer I sat there, the longer my cock wanted to explode. My dominance grew deeper, more powerful. I wanted to shatter the glass in my hand because I was so high in the goddamn clouds.

She hesitated again, like she didn't know what I was asking.

"Touch yourself, Lovely." I could make this woman do anything I wanted, and watching her pleasure herself sounded appealing.

She ran her hands underneath her tits then cupped them, her soft skin sliding over the swell of her breasts. She massaged them, looking awkward in the beginning. But the more she explored herself, the more she enjoyed it. I was watching her own self-discovery, watching her understand her body more.

One hand slid between her legs and found her nub. She rubbed her clit slowly, taking a deep breath at initial contact. She closed her eyes and tilted her head to the side, her hair shifting slightly.

Fuck, I wanted to come.

I stopped drinking my scotch and focused on her instead, on this voluptuous woman at my beck and call.

Her breathing increased, and a tint flushed her skin. Her nipples hardened, and her chest reddened from arousal. She could do what I asked and pretend to enjoy it, but she couldn't force her body to react that way.

She enjoyed every second of it.

And she enjoyed how much pleasure I got out of it.

"On your back. Ass over the edge of the bed." I slammed my glass down and nearly shattered it, my excitement getting the best of me.

When she pulled her fingers away, I caught the stickiness that stretched before it broke apart.

Jesus Christ.

She moved to her back on the edge of the bed with her knees pulled to her chest.

I positioned myself in front of her and placed her feet against my chest, looking down at her like I owned her. With my eyes trained on her, I unbuttoned my shirt and yanked it off. Once her feet touched my bare chest, I moaned. My hands moved for my slacks next and got them undone. I pulled them down, along with my boxers, anxious to get my cock inside of her. I knew how wet that pussy was. I'd been in there once before.

I grabbed her hips and adjusted her underneath me, lining her up perfectly to take my nine inches. "Lovely."

Her hands snaked to my wrists, locking around them like usual. "Yes, sir?"

I closed my eyes and breathed through the pleasure, loving her complete obedience. She was so sexy it was actually torture. "Tell me to eat you out." I knew she liked it last time I did it, and frankly, I fucking loved it. Her pussy was so sweet I could eat it all day.

Instead of a flash of hesitance, her eyes lit up with excitement. She covered it up instantly, but she wasn't quick enough to hide it completely. "Eat my pussy, Crewe."

I leaned over her body and fisted her hair before I gave her a soft kiss. My tongue transferred some scotch to her mouth, the amber liquid moving across both of our tongues. I breathed into her mouth as I felt her perky tits press against my chest. Now that I had her mouth, I didn't want to pull away. She was an incredible kisser. "Yes, Lovely." I broke our kiss and moved to my knees on the hardwood floor. I threw her legs over my shoulders and devoured her, sucking her clit into my mouth and tasting her perfect sweetness.

She was quiet at first, but eventually, she couldn't hide her pleasure. She moaned from the bed and her hands dug into my hair. Her back arched, and she shifted her hips, giving my mouth access to everything.

I could do this all night, and I was tempted to beat off

while I continued to lick and kiss her. Her pussy was a slit of heaven, and I wanted to taste her for lunch and dinner. But my cock was anxious to be inside her, to stretch apart that tight pussy.

I sucked her clit hard into my mouth before I rose to my full height. My arms gripped her by the back of the knees, and I stretched her wide apart. The tip of my cock found her entrance all on its own. I felt the moisture with the head of my cock without even pushing inside.

She wanted this as much as I did.

"Lovely, tell me to fuck you."

Her hands moved to my wrists again. "Fuck me, Crewe." Her lips were swollen from where I kissed her, and her nipples were still hard like diamonds. Her grip around my wrists tightened in anticipation.

I shoved my cock inside her, sliding through the moisture and the tightness. I sunk deep, feeling her walls tighten around me in reaction. Her body slowly acclimated to me, trying to adjust so she could take in every inch of my long length.

She felt as amazing as last time.

I rocked into her slowly, moaning in the back of my

throat as I claimed the woman underneath me. When she first came into my captivity, I found her unremarkable. But now, I thought she was exceptional, the kind of woman I never thought I'd have the honor of meeting until she walked into my life. I'd never bended so hard for someone, went back on my word, or lessened a punishment out of compassion.

She did strange things to me.

My hands left her knees and moved to her tits. I cupped them both as I slowly rocked into her, sliding in and out of her utter perfection. My cock loved being buried inside her just like this. He never wanted to leave.

Her tits were even more perfect. So round and firm. My thumbs brushed over her nipples, flicking the pebbled skin harshly. My eyes locked on hers as I gave her my full length over and over. I could feel her moisture seep down the base of my cock and to my balls as they tapped against her ass. I didn't need to wet myself at all before I entered her.

I wanted to pound into her hard and give it to her as rough as possible. But now that we moved together, I enjoyed the slowness, the sensual movement of our bodies. I loved feeling every inch of her, moving slow enough to savor every second. For the first time, I didn't want to fuck hard.

I just wanted to do this.

The quiet sounds she made got louder as we moved together. Her moans turned to pants. And those pants became quiet screams. Her tits shook every time I thrust into her, moving with my momentum.

"You're fucking beautiful, Lovely." I moved my hand to her throat and rested my fingers over the vulnerable skin. I felt her pulse hammering under the skin, thudding deeply. Her blood pounded in her veins, moving to her heart and then back again. I loved having her in my iron grip.

I bent down and kissed her neck, deepening the angle of my thrusts. My cock reached a more intimate level, hitting her in the right spot that drove all women crazy. My pelvis rubbed against her clit, stimulating it at the same time. My fingers moved to the back of her neck and gripped her tightly. "Tell me to come inside you."

Her mouth moved against mine when I kissed her. "Come inside me…"

I quickened my thrusts, pounding her into the mattress. My

cock moved far inside every time I rocked into her, and I prepared for her release. I could read her breaths and her moans. I'd fucked enough women to know when they were about to come. I edged myself as I waited, knowing she was just seconds from falling over the edge too. "Come for me."

She bit her bottom lip in the sexiest way before she tightened around me. "Oh god…" Her hands moved up my chest and neck until she cupped my face. She pulled my mouth close to hers and breathed with me, her moans notched up to nearly screams. "Crewe…"

I didn't even need to tell her to say that. "Here it comes, Lovely." I'd fantasized about this very moment countless times. I wanted to fill her with so much come that she couldn't walk anywhere without it dripping all over the floor. I wanted her to feel full of me for the rest of the day.

She was still in the midst of her climax, and she dug her nails into my skin as she held on. "Crewe…"

My cock thickened just before release. I shoved myself far inside her, wanting to get every single drop as deep as possible. When the wave of pleasure rolled over my body, I nearly forgot how to breathe. I moaned and crushed my mouth against hers, feeling the heat wash over me. I came hard and long, relishing every minute of the exquisite pleasure. It felt so wonderful, like I owned the world and everyone in it.

Even when I was finished, I kept my cock inside her. I never wanted to leave the warmth of this woman. She was better than any lover I'd ever had, and that was saying something because I had experience with some of the most beautiful and confident women in the world. But there was something about London that satisfied my darkest urges.

I slowly pulled out of her and watched my come seep from her soaked pussy. I admired my handiwork, my claim. "On your hands and knees."

Still breathless and sweaty, she stared at me in surprise.

"You think I'm finished?"

Ariel and I had dinner together at my favorite restaurant in Scotland, The Kitchin. French techniques on Scottish delicacies, it was one of my favorite places in Edinburgh. Ariel didn't eat much of anything, so my choice made no difference to her. Her commitment to being thin baffled me because she was pretty enough to look however she wanted. Personally, I liked curves on a woman. London had the perfect hips, the nice curve in her waist, and gorgeous tits.

I ordered the scallops, and Ariel ordered the halibut. It was difficult not to order seafood when we were so close to the North Sea, the place where fishermen caught fresh fish just that morning.

She and I discussed work, like usual. We didn't touch on topics about our personal lives very often. We had too many other things to discuss on a daily basis. Running two enormous companies, one criminal and one private, sucked the time from both of us.

We drank our wine and ate our entrees, discussing the new shipments of Scotch we sent out to America. They had their own form of scotch, known as bourbon, but most restaurants preferred to keep both selections on hand.

"Our little ploy with Joseph seemed to work." She swirled her wine before she took a sip.

It more than worked. "Yes. She's been very responsive."

"So I hear." Ariel gave me a knowing look, the corner of her mouth raised in a smile. Despite her dislike of London, she didn't say anything harsh about her in my presence. "So, she's finally under control?"

"Absolutely." When I told her to do something, she did it. Sometimes that look came into her eyes, her pure annoyance at the situation she was in. But she obeyed me anyway. That struggle turned me on.

"Are you bringing her to the dinner this Saturday then?"

I stared into my wine before I answered. "Not sure."

"Maybe you should take someone else. Josephine will be there."

I drank the rest of my wine before I set the glass on the table. "I don't care if she's there. I'm not missing an opportunity to speak with Her Majesty. That woman means nothing to me."

Ariel gave me a cold look that suggested she didn't believe me. "I still think you should take someone. The lovelier, the better."

London was the definition of lovely. Those beautiful green eyes would light up the room instantly. In a satin gown handmade by a designer, she would look ravishing. Everyone would see her on my arm and wonder where I found her. She looked like a queen, and she would make me look like a king. "I'll take London. I'm sure she'll be fine."

Ariel raised an eyebrow. "Are you certain of that?"

"Yes." I had her under control.

"Because you have a line of women to choose from."

I did—all of them beautiful, interesting, and smart. "She's at the top of the list."

Ariel cocked her head to the side. "Is she your plaything or something more, Crewe?"

"Plaything," I answered immediately. "You don't have to worry about that."

She seemed to believe me because she looked away. "Good. Because she's a terrible match. American trash. She doesn't know a damn thing about etiquette, how to be a lady, and she certainly doesn't have an ounce of Scottish blood within her."

Ariel's discrimination always amused me. "For a lady, you sure swear a lot."

"Because I'm with you," she reminded me.

"And I don't look Scottish either. Who knows what she is."

"You understood my point, Crewe." She drank her wine again. "Don't act like you didn't. If you want children someday, you can't just pick anyone. You're carrying history in your blood. You're carrying scotch in your blood. Don't fall for an American whore."

"I understand you don't like her, but please don't call her that." I had no reason to defend London and it shouldn't matter to me what Ariel called her, but since I was fucking her every night, I felt obligated to defend her honor. In truth, I really did respect that woman. I didn't initially, but she forced me to with that quick wit and superior intelligence.

Ariel pressed her lips tightly together, ending the conversation. She never apologized for her wrongdoings. She moved forward, her head held high. Not once since we'd been working together did I hear her admit to being at fault for anything.

Her silence was enough. "Thank you."

"So, you're taking her, then?" she asked again. "That's your final decision?"

"Yes."

She pulled out her phone and made a few notes. "I'll arrange for her gown and have Frans take care of her hair and makeup. She is a pretty girl—but we've got to make those features show."

Back to business, like usual. "Her features already show. But now we'll make them pop."

I returned to Stirling Castle late that evening after I finished a meeting in downtown Glasgow. I'd been gone all day, and I wondered what London had been up to since I'd been away. She usually stayed in the bedroom most of the time, wanting to avoid the other men I employed. They were instructed not to touch her unless necessary, but I understood her unease around them when I wasn't near.

I greeted the men in the drawing room before I went upstairs to the royal chambers. I reeked of cigars and scotch, but I liked the smell from time to time. Brought back memories from a long time ago.

I walked inside and found her sitting in the living room, a book in her lap. Her hair was pulled over one shoulder, and her legs were crossed, looking elegant. She hadn't heard the door, so I took the opportunity to stare at her in her natural state.

She licked her fingers before she turned the page, and I found even that arousing. "Hello, Lovely."

Her head snapped and she looked over her shoulder, seeming embarrassed that I caught her off guard. "You were gone for a long time…" She closed the book and left it in her lap.

"Had a few meetings." I sat in the chair beside her, my arm moving over the back of the couch and resting against her neck. She wore leggings and a t-shirt with her hair in a braid. Even in shapeless clothes, she was still beautiful.

She didn't flinch at my proximity. She just accepted it— like she was supposed to. "You smell like a cigar."

"I had a few."

"Smoking is bad for you. Or do Scots not believe that?"

The corner of my mouth rose in a smile. "Didn't realize you cared so much about my well-being."

"I don't." She set the book aside, breaking eye contact with me. "Just hope you don't smell like cigars all the time. Not my favorite scent."

"Have you ever had one?"

"Can't say I have."

"There's a first time for everything, right?"

"I'll pass." She rested her hands in her lap.

I stared at her lips and noticed the plumpness of her mouth. I had kissed her countless times, but I always wanted more. My hand moved to the back of her head, and I held her in place as I leaned in and kissed her. The second I touched her, I felt the electricity course through my veins. Even soft kisses, the tender and sensual kind, brought me to my knees. I wasn't sure if it was her, me, or both of us together.

Her lips moved with mine slowly, slightly trembling at the touch. She took a deep breath, her chest rising against me. When she breathed into my mouth, I felt the heat of her embrace. I knew these kisses made her tremble just the way they made me tremble.

I pulled away then ran my fingers through her hair as I looked her in the eye. "I have a dinner to go to Saturday evening. I'd like you to accompany me."

She opened her mouth to argue or ask questions, but she abruptly closed it again, knowing she didn't have any say in the matter.

I actually pitied her. "You can speak freely." My fingers continued to move through her soft hair, and I realized I missed her. I missed the smartass comments she used to make. I even missed the way she would insult me so easily. I missed the fiery, strong, and fierce woman I abducted months ago.

"What's the catch?" she whispered.

"There is no catch. I want you to be yourself —sometimes."

"How generous of you…" She stared at me coldly.

I leaned in and kissed her again, curious to see what she would do. Like I suspected, she kissed me back with the same passion, the same sexy sensuality as before. Her body always reacted to mine in the same way, like she was susceptible to our chemistry.

It made me wonder if everything she said were just words —forced attitude.

"Ariel has arranged your gown and everything else. We'll leave for Edinburgh late on Saturday afternoon."

"How far is Edinburgh?"

"An hour. Usually less with my driver." I chuckled to myself.

London glanced at my lips, as if she wanted another kiss. "So what is this dinner we're going to?"

"It's for Holyrood Week. That's when Scotland welcomes Her Majesty for a celebration. There is a parade during the day, festivities in the afternoon, and then the grand dinner later at the Palace of Holyroodhouse. Lord Provost of Scotland will recognize Scotland residents for their remarkable achievements throughout the year."

Her jaw popped open in shock. "Are you serious?"

"Yes." My fingers continued to explore her hair, obsessed with it.

"Like, this is a royal event?"

"I suppose." I'd been doing these sorts of things all my life. I took them for granted.

"So...are you like a prince or something?"

"God, no," I said with a scoff. "And don't ever call me one. I'm related to the royal family, but I have no function in parliament."

She still looked confused. "I don't understand."

"The Queen of England is the leader of England, but she's actually just a figurehead. The prime minister is actually in charge of all matters as head of state. Same thing."

"Oh, I guess…" She fidgeted with her fingers like she couldn't sit still. "I don't think I'm the best person to take to this sort of thing." Since I'd given her a grace period, she didn't have to obey me without question. "I don't know anything about the customs or even how to curtsy."

"You don't have to curtsy to anyone. A handshake is fine."

"I can shake the queen's hand?" she asked incredulously.

"It would be awfully rude if you didn't since I'm going to introduce you."

"Oh my god…" She covered her mouth with her hand like she could hardly believe it. "I don't know if this is such a good idea. I'm going to embarrass you."

I leaned in and kissed the corner of her mouth, feeling her melt at my touch. "You could never embarrass me. You're absolutely beautiful."

For the first time ever, her expression softened. She looked at me with slightly parted lips and friendly eyes. There were no walls around her heart and soul. There were no games, no defenses. But once the moment passed, the fortifications returned once again. "I just…I don't know how to act. I don't know what to say."

"I'll be there with you. So don't worry about it."

"Why don't you take one of your regulars?" Her tone hardened toward the end.

I cocked my head to the side. "Is that jealousy again?"

"For the last time, I'm not jealous."

"I think you are." I smiled because I enjoyed the idea of her growing upset when she pictured me with other women. "And I don't want to take them. I want to take you."

"Not even your French diplomat?"

I told her about Sasha? I couldn't even recall the conversation. And if I couldn't remember it, it was a shock that she did. "Sasha?"

"Whatever her name is," she said coldly. "Wouldn't you want to take her to this thing?"

"She's already met the queen—multiple times. And no, I'd rather take you."

"Do I get a say in this?"

My fingers moved to her neck. "No." I gave her a firm stare, telling her there was no way around it. "You can bitch and moan, though. Until I tell you your time is up."

London knew complaining was a waste of time. "I'm nervous."

"Don't be. Just be yourself."

"So I should walk in there and tell everyone that I'm being held against my will?" She challenged, being the smartass she was.

I missed that fiery attitude. "If you did, I think everyone would assume you were crazy."

"Not if they know you…"

I leaned in and gave her another kiss, wanting something to hold me over while I showered. "I'm going to shower. When I get out, we're back to what we were."

She kissed me with the same sensuality even though she didn't have to.

And that really made me feel like a king.

LONDON

He finished up in the bathroom then walked into the bedroom, a towel wrapped around his waist. Drops of water still glistened on his chest, and his hair was still damp. He was all muscle and power.

I tried not to stare.

He'd been gone all day and all night. When he walked in the door, it was almost midnight. He said he had worked all day, but in the back of my mind, I wondered if that was really true. Was he spending time with his regulars? He said he had a few in Glasgow. I'd have to be really dense to think our arrangement would change his promiscuity.

He dropped the towel, his ass looking nice and tight. He

pulled on a fresh pair of boxers and nothing else since he was going to bed soon. And he slept in the nude, so the boxers weren't really necessary either.

I sat at the edge of the bed and tried to ignore his obvious hotness.

He crawled on the bed and came up behind me, his face moving into my neck with decadent kisses. Hot breaths filled my ear, and he yanked my t-shirt over my shoulder, exposing more skin to caress.

As much as I hated being bossed around all the time, I did love his affection. The sex was good, and I got as much out of it as he did. If I weren't attracted to him, this would be scarring. But since I was satisfied every night with the tender caresses, it really wasn't that bad.

It was important to remain positive.

Joseph would come for me, or I would make my escape. I just had to be patient.

Crewe pulled me down on the bed then leaned over me, so he was upside down. He sprinkled kisses along my chin, his face cleanly shaven. His lips moved to mine, and he gave me a soft kiss, the kind that made my toes curl.

His touch felt nice, but then an image of Sasha came into

my mind, a beautiful woman that I could never compare to. I moved from underneath him and sat up. "I want to ask you something."

He gave me an ice-cold look. "You don't get to ask me anything unless I give you my permission."

When he was dominant like this, there was nothing I could do but listen. I had to bite back the retort on my tongue and not slap him across the face. I had to submit, to surrender. "And do I have your permission?"

He pulled me back to the bed then adjusted me underneath him. My clothes were still on, so he yanked my top off then unclasped my bra with a single hand. "Make it quick." He yanked off my leggings and took my panties with them.

When I looked at his hard body, I felt my own become soft and wet. My pussy throbbed for his definition to fill me. I wanted to deny that I enjoyed being manipulated into sex, but I couldn't do it anymore. It was the best sex I'd ever had. "Were you with another woman tonight?"

He pulled off his boxers, showing his throbbing cock. He gave me an aggressive look, like the question displeased him. "What does it matter?"

"Because I don't want to catch anything. So if you're

sleeping around, then I have the right to ask for a condom."

"You don't have the right to do anything." He yanked me underneath him and positioned himself on top of me. He rocked his hips and rubbed his cock through my slickness. He leaned down and dragged his tongue across the valley between my tits, kissing my neck at the very end. "I will fuck you exactly how I want to fuck you." He shoved his cock violently inside me, stretching my insides without giving my body any warning.

I gripped his biceps automatically and laid back, enjoying just how full he made me. "Just answer me…" I was losing focus with this Scottish king on top of me.

"Answer." He thrust into me. "What?" He pinned me to the mattress and shoved himself deep inside me, hitting my favorite sweet spot and making my knees shake. His hand fisted the back of my hair as he kept me still, his hips working hard to fuck me.

"Were you with someone else tonight?" I had to know the answer.

He sank into me then remained still on top of me. "What I do is none of your business. If I fuck other women, it's none of your business."

"I just want to—"

"Shut up." His dark gaze bored into mine as he rocked into me again. "Don't ask me again. Do you understand?"

I would never get my answer, and I felt a twinge of pain when I didn't. Was it jealousy? Was it purely for health reasons? Or did I just want to know more about him? More about my enemy? "Yes, sir."

"Good." Sweat formed on his chest as he pounded into me. "Now fuck me, Lovely."

When I woke up the following morning, Crewe was gone. He was never there in the morning, always somewhere else in the castle with the rest of his men. Sometimes he went into town for meetings. He was a busy man with a packed schedule.

I was tired of sitting inside this bedroom. I had a beautiful world right outside my window, but I wasn't making the most of it. It wasn't a resort with a pool and spa, but it had beautiful courtyards and a thousand rooms to explore.

I'd been stuck in here the entire time.

I ignored the breakfast tray sitting outside my door and walked downstairs in my active wear. I was desperate to stretch my legs and get my blood going in a different way besides sex. When I reached the entryway, Dunbar spotted me. "You aren't making another run for it, bitch."

I wanted to break his nose. "I'm just looking for Crewe."

He walked toward me at the bottom of the stairs, looking terrifying with the scar on his face. He wore a black leather jacket with a gun on his hip and a blade. "Get your ass back to your room." He snatched me by the elbow and yanked me with more force than necessary.

I twisted out of his grasp then slammed my hand into his nose. "Don't touch me."

He growled when he began to bleed then slapped me so hard across the face I flew to the ground. "You wanna play rough, cunt? Then we'll play rough."

I scooted away so he couldn't grab me again, ignoring the burning pain on my cheek. "Crewe told you not to touch me like that."

"Well, you're trying to run away." He stepped toward me then grabbed me by the ankle. "Rules no longer apply." He yanked me hard across the stone floor, chaffing my skin across the grooves.

Dunbar smiled as he watched me struggle.

I did the only thing I could do. "Crewe!" I yelled at the top of my lungs, hoping he was still on the grounds and could hear me.

"He's gone for the afternoon." He yanked hard on my leg and forced my body to turn. "So, it's just you and—"

"Let. Her. Go." Crewe's voice was amplified in the enormous room, reaching the top of the vaulted ceiling. His footsteps could be heard now that Dunbar had stopped breathing and pulling on my leg.

Dunbar immediately dropped me. "She was trying to run again."

"I was not!" He wasn't looking, so I slammed my foot into his shin.

"Fuck!" He hopped away then pulled his shin to his chest. "Cunt!"

"There's plenty more where that came from, asshole." Of all Crewe's men, I hated him the most. And I desperately missed Finley, the one person who actually showed me some respect. Ariel was a bitch, but she didn't lay a hand on me.

Crewe came to my side and looked down at me, his

expression cold. "Were you trying to escape?" The implication of my actions filled the air between us.

"No."

"Then why are you dressed like that?" He nodded to my workout gear.

"I was going to ask you if I could visit the grounds or go on a run or something." I checked my leg to make sure it wasn't sprained before I rose to my feet. "I'm tired of being cooped up in that room all day."

When Crewe's hostility dropped, I knew he believed me. "You can visit the grounds with Dunbar."

That was worse than staying in my room all day. "Crewe, I'm not going to run again—"

"Don't insult me," he said coldly. "If the opportunity ever presents itself, we both know you'll take it. Dunbar will escort you." He turned to walk away like the conversation was over.

"Wait." I caught up to him and hooked my arm through his, touching him for the first time that day. I felt the strength of his arms the moment we embraced. Just last night, that powerful body was on top of me, pressing me hard into the mattress. "He makes me uncomfortable." I knew Dunbar would do something more sinister if he had the opportunity. He didn't see me as Crewe's woman—just his prisoner.

"Then go to your room." He stared at me beside him, his expression still cold.

"Could you come with me?" Even though Crewe was the reason I was here at all, he was the only person I felt comfortable with. He would never hurt me—not seriously. And when he kissed me and fucked me, I enjoyed it. "I don't like him." I rose on my tiptoes and gave him a kiss, feeling the stubble along his chin and jaw.

He kissed me back immediately, his lips moving slowly with mine.

I pulled away, feeling the burn of my mouth the moment we touched. I wanted to keep going, but Dunbar was staring.

When he looked at me, his gaze was a little softer. "I'm a busy man, Lovely. I can't babysit you all day."

"I know but—"

"Ariel can watch you. Is that better?"

She wouldn't hurt me, but she wasn't much better. "You must work out sometimes. Can I come with you then?"

"You couldn't keep up with me."

My eyes narrowed in offense. "You'd be surprised."

"Actually, I'd be shocked if you could."

The sexist comment unnerved me, but my attraction still lingered. "I accept your challenge."

His hand snaked around my waist, and he pulled me into his chest, not caring about anyone who may be watching. He pressed his mouth to mine and kissed me hard, his hand digging deep into my hair.

He took my breath away.

He released me then walked away.

"Can I accompany you today? Wherever you go, I go."

He turned around, his black suit fitting the contours of his body perfectly. "I'm a very busy man. And you're a distraction."

"I'll be quiet."

"No." His voice turned cold. "Ariel will take you out for an hour a day. That's it."

"Crewe, I'm not a fucking dog." I hated this treatment. I didn't have any rights or any options. All I wanted was to spend time outside in the sunlight, and I couldn't even have that. "I need more than that. At Fair Isle, I got to spend all day outside. You're torturing me by keeping me cooped up in there."

"You're a prisoner," he barked. "So just get used to it."

My hand ached to slap that attitude right out of him. "How about—"

"Silence." When his eyes turned black, I knew he wasn't fucking around. "Say another goddamn word and see what happens." The threat filled the air, my brother's life in danger once again.

As much as it killed me, I remained quiet.

"On your knees."

I hated obeying like a dog. I hated having no rights. All I could do was listen to this madman boss me around. But when my family was on the line, I would do anything— even the things I venomously despised.

I moved to my knees.

Crewe stared at me with a hard expression, the approval showing in his eyes. He slowly walked toward me, closing the gap between us until he was directly in front of me. Without taking his eyes off my face, he commanded Dunbar. "Leave us."

Dunbar's footsteps trailed away as he left the entryway room and disappeared to another part of the castle.

Crewe undid his belt then loosened his slacks, his eyes trained on me. He pulled down the brim of his boxers so his cock could be free, long and hard with a bulging vein running through it. The tip was darker than the rest of the shaft, swollen with blood. "Suck me off, Lovely." His hand moved into my hair, and he gathered it in his fingertips before he fisted it.

I'd never sucked his cock before. I hadn't given a blowjob in a long time, since my last boyfriend years ago. The problem was, Crewe was much bigger than any man I'd ever taken. Must be that Scottish blood.

He grabbed himself by the base and stroked his thumb along the surface. He pressed his head against my lips, rubbing the warm skin against my mouth. A drop formed at the tip then smeared across my lips like Chap-Stick.

I opened my mouth and swiped my tongue over the head, collecting anything I may have missed. The taste of salt and his arousal filled my mouth, and my pussy clenched in response. I licked him again then opened my jaw as wide as I could. My neck craned to take him inch by inch. He lowered himself and entered my mouth, working his way down until he was deep in my throat.

I nearly gagged.

Crewe closed his eyes and moaned. "Lovely, your mouth feels so good…" He rocked his hips slowly, entering my mouth deeply until he pulled out again. He wasn't vicious with me like I expected, seeming to understand he had a big cock to take.

I flattened my tongue and moved with him, taking his cock over and over. I took a breath when I got the chance then wrapped my hand around his base. I stroked him at the same time as he entered my mouth, his swollen head moving deep into the back of my throat. My saliva dripped down his length and onto my hand, giving me more lubrication to stroke him.

Crewe pumped into my throat at a greater pace, entering me deep and hard. He breathed deeply as I pleasured him, his brown eyes vibrant. His hand moved to the back of my neck where he got a good grip. "I can't wait to come in your mouth, Lovely."

To my surprise, I wanted to taste him too. I tightened my

grip on his dick and stroked him harder, my mouth working at the same time. My neck ached from the constant movement, and my knees burned from the way I was sitting, but nothing slowed me down.

His fingertips dug into my skin, and a quiet moan escaped his throat. "Here it comes." He shoved himself far into the back of my throat, nearly initiating my gag reflex a few times. He viciously pumped into me as he got off. He released a loud moan and shoved himself in as far as he would go, dumping everything inside me.

Mounds of his come hit the back of my throat and dripped down, oozing everywhere. I could taste some on the back of my tongue, and I noticed a hint of salt, among other things. I watched his expression as he gave me everything he had, his eyes locked to mine with possessiveness.

When he was finished, he slowly pulled out of me and returned his dick to his pants. "Show me."

I wasn't entirely sure what he meant, but I stuck out my tongue.

He gave me a look of approval. "Swallow."

Most of it had already slid down my throat, so I consumed the rest of it.

His eyes darkened before he extended a hand and helped me up. "Ariel will come by your room when she's ready."

What? That was it? My panties were soaked after I watched him get off. He always took care of me, so the jarring goodbye was off-putting. "How about you come with me back to the room?"

His hand moved to my neck, his favorite place to touch me. "No. This way, you'll be thinking about me all day."

I already did think about him all day, whether it was fantasies of killing him or fucking him.

He kissed me on the mouth even though I just sucked him off. Then he abruptly let me go and walked away, back to work as if I hadn't just sucked his cock in the entryway of an ancient castle.

***

Ariel sat on the cushioned arm chair with her tablet, her black glasses resting on the bridge of her nose. Her eye makeup gave her a mysterious look, and the designer clothes she wore made her look more like a model than a businesswoman. She glanced at me from time to time but didn't say a word to me.

262 | PENELOPE SKY

I enjoyed the sight of the trees and the tulips, letting the sun soak into my skin and make me feel warm. The walls of the castle surrounded us, shifting and turning across the green land. In the distance were more trees and hills, the surroundings just as beautiful. The air was different here, cleaner and lighter.

Everything I'd seen of Scotland had been beautiful. Even Fair Isle, out in the middle of the North Sea, was breathtaking. Freezing and windy, it was still a sight to behold. And now I was seeing a structure that was so old I couldn't comprehend it.

I wasn't sure how safe I felt with Ariel. If one of the other men tried to take advantage of me, I didn't think she would do anything to protect me. But she was loyal to Crewe, so I assumed she would do as he asked. But even then, she didn't carry a gun. Crewe claimed she was the toughest of them all, so maybe she had hidden talents I didn't know about.

Her attitude was definitely ruthless.

I walked through the courtyard then ventured to the other side, spotting a squirrel in the tree.

"Don't go too far." The warning in Ariel's voice told me not to challenge her.

I watched the squirrel until he disappeared, and then I returned to the clearing. The tulips in the flower bed were different colors: pink, yellow, blue, and every other color you could think of. The climate of Scotland made summer feel like spring. It was a nice change compared to the blistering heat of New York.

But I still missed that humidity.

I wondered if my friends had given up searching for me. I wondered if NYU had pulled my name out for semester and replaced me with someone else. I wondered if the police had given up their search and I was just another cold case. I'd been gone for two and a half months. That was a long time for a person to be missing. Everyone probably thought I was chopped up into tiny pieces in the harbor.

"I found a squirrel," I explained to her. "I was just watching him." I didn't owe her an explanation, but I didn't want her to think I was trying to slip away. I already did that once before, and I got my ass whooped. The sensation was difficult to understand because I both liked it and hated it. I loved how aroused Crewe was. I loved how he ate me out with a mouth that knew exactly what it was doing. But I hated the marks on my ass the next day. After applying ointment for a week, the marks finally faded away.

"I don't give a damn what you were doing," she said harshly. "Don't cross me." She looked up from her tablet and gave me a cold stare with her blue eyes. The black frames sitting on her nose made her look more intimidating than she already was. "I shouldn't be out here on toddler duty." She pressed her lips tightly together and shook her head. "With all the shit I do for that man, I can't believe he would lower me to such a pitiful task."

How did Crewe work with this woman all day, every day? She was absolutely horrendous. I'd never seen her crack a smile or make a joke. While Crewe was intense, he had a sense of humor. He smiled at some of the things I said. "In his defense, I said I didn't trust his men, so he sent you."

She sighed in pure frustration. "I think you should trust me even less."

"You don't look interested in women, so I think I'm okay."

"There are worse things than being raped," she said

coldly. "I'm sure you know that by now. But then again, you've never been raped."

The relationship I had with Crewe was wrong, but I didn't necessarily see him as a bad person. When I said I didn't want to sleep with him, he respected my wishes. Every time we were together, it was mutual. I admit I was here against my will, that I had to obey him even though I didn't want to, but the sex was something I actually enjoyed. Being trapped here is the part I despised. "You hate me, right?"

"Absolutely." She turned her gaze back to her tablet. "You're just a distraction for Crewe. He has more important things to do than keep a pet all day."

"Well…why don't you just turn a blind eye and let me go?" She wouldn't have to deal with me ever again. She wouldn't have to look at my face or hear my voice. Crewe could go back to working at his full potential. "We both win."

She looked up again, her eyes piercing through the lenses. "As much as I would love to do that, I'm very loyal to my employer. I'll tell him to his face that he needs to either kill you or let you go. But I won't go against his wishes behind his back. I respect that man a great deal."

"Yet, you treat me like shit," I pointed out.

She lowered the tablet in her lap, obviously finished with whatever she was doing. "I've made my feelings for you very clear. But Crewe defends your honor every time. He can be a gentleman in the most unexpected ways."

For some reason, that meant a lot to me. Crewe had my back when I wasn't even in the room. When one of his men grabbed me, he was there to protect me. When Ariel insulted me, he defended me. "He doesn't make any sense. He has so many soft spots, but he can be so hard at the same time."

"Crewe is a very complicated man. He's compassionate because he's suffered more than most. But he's unsympathetic to people who don't take control of their fate the way he did."

I wanted to know more about Crewe and his past. This was the second time this had come up. "What happened to him?"

"I'm not at liberty to say. If he wants to tell you, he will."

I was the only one in the dark. "Does Crewe still sleep with his regulars?" Crewe wouldn't answer my question even though I'd asked him several times, but I still wanted an answer.

She narrowed her eyes, nearly offended. "Why are you asking me that?"

"You know everything about him, right?"

"I try to stay out of his sex life," she said coldly. "None of my business."

"But you like to mention me to him."

Her coldness didn't thaw. "Are you jealous?" She crossed her arms over her chest and cocked her head to the side. "Because you do understand you're just his plaything, not his lover. If he wants to sleep around, he will. It's none of your concern."

"I understand what I am to him. But I deserve all the facts."

"Then ask him yourself." She lowered her arms back to her lap.

I would have to. No one was willing to give me any answers around here. I was important enough to keep but not important enough to share information with. It wasn't like I was asking for banking information. "I'm nervous for this dinner on Saturday. I told him he shouldn't take me but he wants to anyway."

She sighed loudly. "I don't have a clue why he's taking you either. Sasha is perfect for these sorts of things."

I hated that name. It was like grinding a rock against my teeth.

"But Crewe always gets what he wants," she said with another sigh. "I'll make sure you look your best so you don't embarrass yourself."

It didn't matter how good I looked. I would probably embarrass myself anyway.

Crewe returned to the royal chambers late that evening. I had dinner alone and was ready to go to bed. Since I got to spend the afternoon outside, I was no longer restless.

He walked in the door, smelling like cigars again. He greeted me with a look as he loosened his tie. He headed to the bathroom as more articles of clothing fell onto the floor.

I could tell he wasn't in the mood to talk, so I didn't ask him anything. But I picked up his clothes off the floor and placed them on the hanger so one of the maids would take them to be dry cleaned tomorrow. I didn't know anything about suits, but I knew his clothes must be expensive and well made. I wasn't sure why I cared at all. The well-being of his clothes shouldn't matter. He obviously didn't care about my well-being as a human.

After he showered, he came back into the bedroom with a towel wrapped around his waist. His chest glistened with the remaining water drops that fell from his hair and down his shoulders. He stopped when he spotted the suit hanging from the back of the door, but he didn't comment on it.

"You really shouldn't smoke." I wasn't trying to pick a fight with him, but the smell from his clothes bothered me.

"I thought you didn't care about me."

"I don't, but I don't want you to get lung cancer."

He grabbed a pair of boxers from his drawer and looked at me, the corner of his mouth raising in a smile. "That's an interesting contradiction. You don't care about me, but you want me to live as long as possible. Interesting."

"I'm just saying that as a friend."

"So we're friends?" He pulled on his boxers and walked around the bed until we were face to face. That arrogant smile was still on his lips. Sometimes, when it was just the two of us, he showed me a side of him that he didn't let anyone else see. He was playful, even funny.

"No. I just…" I didn't know how to dig myself out of the conversational hole I'd just gotten into.

"We aren't friends." He came closer to me, the drops on his skin glistening. "Friends don't fuck the way we do." He leaned toward me and kissed the corner of my mouth, his body wash sweeping over me.

I forgot what I was saying and melted at the touch, feeling his lips with my own. He chased away everything when we embraced. I didn't think about my brother, my imprisonment, or anything else.

He pulled away, our lips sticking together just before they broke apart. "Ariel told me she had a great time today."

I rolled my eyes. "Liar."

He chuckled then walked to the table where he kept his scotch. The maid brought a fresh bucket of ice every night so he could drink his booze the way he liked. He poured himself a glass then took a long drink before he returned the glass to the table. "She's still not your biggest fan."

"What a coincidence," I said sarcastically. "I don't care for her either."

He poured another glass.

"You drink too much." One a day is fine, but he must have had twelve glasses a day. Ironically, I'd never seen him drunk. Unless he was drunk all the time, and I'd never known him sober.

He ignored my observation and took another drink. "She said you're nosy."

"Nosy?"

"Asking about my past and my women."

I didn't like the way he referred to them possessively. It made my spine tense in annoyance. "She brought up your past first. So that doesn't count."

"Then why are you asking about the other one?" He drank from his glass again before he finally set it down.

"How can you drink like that?"

"Why do you care?" He licked his lips just to get another taste.

"I don't think I've ever seen you drink water."

272 | PENELOPE SKY

"You've seen me drink coffee."

"Is that water?" I couldn't keep my attitude back. It always leaked out when I spoke to him.

He smiled, amused. "You don't like it when I smoke. You don't like it when I drink—"

"I don't care if you drink. You just drink too much."

"Whatever," he said. "And you don't like it when I sleep with other women. Hmm...that's very interesting." He stood in front of me, staring me down with those warm brown eyes. "Sounds like you're pretty fond of me."

"I'm not fond of you. If I could leave right now, I would."

"Really?" he challenged. "I'm not sure if I believe that anymore."

"Then destroy that detonator, and I'll prove it."

He stared me down without saying a word.

"The only reason why I want to know about other women you're bedding is because I don't want to catch something disgusting. I was clean before I met you, and I intend to stay that way." My request wasn't unfair. I had the right to know about my own health.

"I'm clean, Lovely."

"But if you're sleeping around—"

"Like I said before, that's none of your concern."

I wanted to scream. "Fine. Then let's use condoms."

He laughed like the request was absurd. "No."

"Does that mean you are sleeping around?" I narrowed my eyes. "All I'm looking for is an answer, not an explanation. I don't care if you are screwing other women. Just use a condom with them, at least."

"Bullshit," he said. "You do care. I can tell just by looking at you."

I swallowed my anger. "I don't. But even if I did, what does it matter? It shouldn't change your answer."

"And it doesn't. I don't talk about my life with anyone. You aren't special."

For some reason, that response actually did hurt. I couldn't put my finger on exactly why. He slept with me every night, he fucked me every day, and he was the only person on this side of the world I felt somewhat safe with. When I was with him, nothing worse could happen to me.

I turned around so I wouldn't have to look at him anymore. It gave me a chance to collect my emotions so they wouldn't appear on my face. "Since you have this obvious leverage over me, why can't I go outside on my own? If I run away, you'll kill Joseph. Obviously, I won't let that happen, so I'm not going to go anywhere. Whether I'm being supervised or not, I'm still your prisoner." I turned back around, my arms across my chest. I gave him a stoic expression, hiding the hurt I felt deep inside.

He walked to the bed and pulled down the covers then set his alarm on his phone. "You have a good point."

"Is that a yes?"

He sat with his back against the headboard, his cock hardening as it rested against his stomach. "I'll think about it."

That was the most I was going to get out of him.

"Come here." His voice turned authoritative, his desire obvious in the heat of his gaze. His cock hardened further, becoming nine inches of steel. "Clothes off. Now."

Seeing his naked body made my own grow wet. I dropped my shirt and bottoms then straddled his hips. I hadn't been on top since the night I tried to seduce him. His enormous cock lay underneath me, warm and thick.

His hands went to my hips, and he moved his face between my tits. He sucked each of my nipples into his mouth, biting them slightly before his tongue moved over them in apology. He moved to my neck and kissed me everywhere, his cock throbbing anxiously to be inside me. "I thought you would be anxious for my cock the second I walked through the door." His hands glided all over my body, touching me everywhere. His lips caressed my soft skin then brushed against my ear.

The moment I was alone, I touched myself and found my release. I knew I wouldn't be able to last all day waiting for him. My hands dug into his hair as I grinded against him, forgetting about the hurt and the anger I felt toward him. When our bodies collided like this, I didn't think about anything.

He pulled away and looked at me. "Lovely." His hands gripped my ass and pulled my cheeks apart. "Did you touch yourself while I was gone?"

The direct question was awkward. No one had ever asked me that before.

"And if you did, did you think about me?"

That question was worse because the answer was humiliating.

"Answer honestly," he threatened. "I'll know if you're lying to me." He looked into my eyes and watched my expression. Like I was a specimen under the microscope, he watched me intently. His voice came out with more authority. "Answer me."

"Yes."

"Yes, what?"

"Yes, I touched myself."

"And?" His warm breath fell on my face.

"I thought of you…"

He closed his eyes and moaned quietly, his fingers digging into my skin. "Lovely…" He lifted my hips and directed me onto his length, my pussy gushing all over his cock. I was just as wet as always. There was no point in hiding my arousal when it was this obvious. He moaned again as he entered me, enjoying my slick tightness. "Fuck me hard." He leaned against the headboard and guided me up and down with his hands.

I rocked my hips and took his length over and over, riding his cock as fast as I could. I held onto his shoulders for balance and felt my tits shake with my movements. My body slickened with sweat, and my temperature rose. I began to moan without even realizing it, knowing this man was better than any fantasy I ever had.

"Keep it up." He thrust his hips underneath me, pounding into me from below. We both worked hard to move together, to give and get as much pleasure as possible. His hand gripped my tit, and he twisted my nipple lightly, making me wince and moan at the same time. "Say my name."

"Crewe…"

He clenched his jaw in arousal, loving the control he had over me. His powerful arms worked to help me move so I could continue at the pace he enjoyed. He grabbed my thighs and tilted my hips, making me rub against him in a different way. "Like this, Lovely."

I could feel my clit rub against his pelvic bone. And it felt so amazing.

He kissed me as we moved together, my breaths coming out shaky as the pleasure ripped through me. I loved everything about this position. I loved his hands on my hips, his lips against mine, his throbbing cock deep inside me, and the way my sensitive nub rubbed against his powerful body.

"Crewe, I'm gonna come…"

"I know," he breathed into my mouth. "Your pussy is fucking tight."

I moved my hips as much as possible, getting as much of his length as I could. And then without warning, I exploded. I came all over his length, my slickness gushing around his cock, and I screamed loud enough for everyone in the castle to hear.

Crewe watched my face, his fingers digging into me. "You're beautiful when you come." He continued to thrust his hips underneath me, giving me his cock to make the climax last forever.

I enjoyed the high and I rode it to the very end, feeling my body tense and relax as the pleasure entered and left my extremities. Now I wanted to take his come the way I took it earlier—just in a new place.

"I want to watch you come again." He moved forward and laid me back on the bed, my head hitting the sheets. His cock remained inside me as he positioned himself between my thighs. Then he fucked me harder than I fucked him, his cock sliding through his come. "And I want you to say my name again."

CREWE

I woke up early that morning and went for a run. I had a big day ahead of me. I had to meet with one of my filtration masters and then attend the Holyrood Week celebration in Edinburgh.

It was a lot to do in a single day.

I showered in a different bedroom in the castle then met with my filtrations master. He did most of his work on the other side of Scotland, and this was the only availability he had for the week. Ariel was there, overseeing things as usual.

When he left, she and I spoke in private.

"What do you think of him?" I asked.

"He's quality," she said. "His family owned a farm fifteen years ago, but they lost it due to the downfall of cotton. He worked as a scotch apprentice in the warehouse in his youth, so he turned to that to support his family. He has a lot of experience, and he really understands how much determination it takes to make something work. I trust his work."

That's why I kept Ariel around. She did her research, and she could read people very well. The only exception to that was London. She never gave my lover the chance she deserved. If she dropped her prejudice, she would probably be fond of her. "Alright. We'll offer him the position for the factory in Edinburgh."

"Got it." She made the note on her tablet. "Frans just arrived at the estate. He's getting London ready."

"Good." I was sure she was giving him an earful about it.

"I found this lovely dress from Valentino. The colors and style will look perfect on her."

"I'm sure. You have great taste." I'd never seen Ariel wear anything besides black, but she did have a knack for these sorts of things.

"Thank you. If we're done here, lunch is ready."

"Good. I'm starving."

When it was time to leave, I walked upstairs and to the royal quarters on the east side. I opened the door without knocking, seeing Frans standing with London in front of the full length mirror in the living room.

"You look beautiful." Frans fluffed out the bottom of the gown, which jutted out around her hips. It was tight around her waist, shaping her curves and leading to a sweetheart neckline that accentuated her perfect breasts. The material was gold with an subtle shine, not sparkly with rhinestones or jewels. The fabric was different than anything I'd ever seen.

She hadn't seen me yet because she was absorbed with her appearance in the mirror. With large curls that reminded me of a beautiful woman from the twenties, her curtain of hair was pulled over one shoulder and pinned with a diamond hairclip. Her cheekbones were highlighted with subtle blush, and her eyes were detailed and smoky, making them appear far greener than they really were. Her complexion was flawless, amplifying her already perfect skin. Everything about her was perfect, screaming royalty like she'd been born into it. I leaned against the frame of the doorway and took the opportunity to admire her, taking advantage of it for as long as I could.

I could stare at her all day.

"Wow." She looked into the mirror with surprise. "Frans, I don't know how you did it. I haven't looked this good since my junior prom. And even then, I didn't look all that great." She was the only one who chuckled at her joke. Since she was obviously beautiful, I doubt Frans could believe that.

"I can't make an ugly woman beautiful," he said with his deep Scottish accent. "But I can make a beautiful woman radiant." He gripped her shoulders gently and gave her a smile in the reflection of the mirror. "His Royal Highness will lose his breath when he looks at you."

"I already have."

London turned at the sound of my voice, obviously having no clue I'd been standing there. Her eyes locked on mine, and she suddenly seemed self-conscious even though she looked nothing short of beautiful.

Frans greeted me with a bow before he shook my hand. "The Duke of Rothesay, it's such a pleasure to see you again."

"The pleasure is mine, Frans. Thank you for making my date look divine."

"I didn't do anything," he said with a chuckle. "That's all her." He gave London a hug before he walked out.

When we were alone together, I closed the gap between us and admired her. My hand moved to the crook of her arm, and I felt her utterly soft skin. My eyes trailed up her body until our eyes locked. "You look beautiful."

"Thanks. I don't think you've ever said that to me before."

"I say it all the time." I just said it yesterday.

"When we're in bed, yes. Not outside of it."

I never noticed before. My hands moved to her slender waistline, and I held her next to me, wanting to take off that dress and move deep inside her. But that would have to wait until later. "Are you ready to go?"

"I think so…Duke." She smiled like she was teasing me. "You told me you didn't have a title."

"I told you I wasn't a prince. Prince is a pussy word."

She rolled her eyes. "Is not. But whatever."

"Yes, I'm a duke. But it's just a title. It doesn't mean anything."

"I think it means a lot."

It didn't mean as much as she thought, and she would never know why. "The car is waiting for us. Let's get going. And remember." I pulled the useless tracker out of my pocket. "Try anything stupid, and you know what happens."

She was just glowing a moment before, but now her face fell in sadness. "You think I ever forget?"

———

The parade ended hours ago, so we pulled into the large roundabout that led to the amazing landmark known as the Holyrood Palace. The garden party would take place within the enclosure of the beautiful building.

When we pulled up to the front, London looked out the window and examined the wonderful arches on the ground floor that led to the inner depths of the palace. Bowls of flowers hung from every other arch, and the large windows on the second floor looked over the entryway and the courtyard on the other side. I'd been here countless times, but I still found the ancient landmark to be fascinating.

"Wow…" When the driver came to her side of the car and opened the door, she forgot to step out. "It's beautiful."

"I know." I gave her a gentle pat on the thigh so she knew to exit.

London took Dunbar's hand, even though she despised him, and stepped out. Other parliament officials mingled together outside the entrance, probably discussing the parade from the afternoon.

I approached from behind her then extended my arm.

It took her a moment to realize what I was asking. She took my arm and held herself with elegance, the way Frans taught her. She kept her shoulders back, her chest up, and she blended in with everyone else.

She turned her lips to my ear. "Do I look nervous?"

"No. You look beautiful."

She released the air she was holding, relaxing slightly.

I guided her to the entrance but stopped to say hello to Lord Provost. I introduced him to London and we made small talk for a few moments before we continued onward. Next, I ran into the First Minister of Scotland, Nicola Sturgeon. I made the introductions, and we discussed a few matters of the scotch business before I continued forward.

"The President of Scotland is a woman?" London asked in surprise.

"Yes. Why is that strange?"

"In America, we'd be lucky to ever have a female president. So far, it's never happened."

I tried not to insult other people's countries. It was in my royal blood. "Hopefully, it'll happen someday. Nicola has been the First Minister for three years now. She's done an excellent job." I continued speaking in my Scottish accent now that we were among the monarchs of the United Kingdom.

She smiled. "I think you sound cute when you talk like that."

"Cute?" Cute was an insult for a guy like me.

"Sexy. Is that better?"

I stopped walking and stared at her, caught by surprise from her compliment. She never said anything nice to me, except when she showed her concern about my drinking and smoking. And even then, she claimed she didn't give a damn about me. "You think I'm sexy?"

She rolled her eyes. "Let's not play games anymore, Crewe."

"I wasn't playing them to begin with." I stared her down, watching her expression.

"We both know I'm attracted to you. I think that's pretty obvious."

"Doesn't mean I don't like hearing it." I continued to walk forward with London still on my arm. Now I wished we could have a moment alone together, even if it was just to share a heated kiss. But that would have to wait until later.

***

I introduced London to a lot of people and explained a lot of titles she would have to write down if she ever had any hope of memorizing them. I only knew these things because of my early childhood.

When I introduced her to the queen, London hid her nerves well. She smiled like she belonged there, greeted her correctly, and even shared a few words with her about the beauty of the palace.

I'd known the queen for a short period of time, since she was simply so much older than me. But I could tell when she adored someone—as rarely as it happened. And she had genuine affection for this woman she'd just met.

The queen and I shared a few more words before we took our seats in the outside garden. Overhead lights streamed across the tables, and the garden was blooming with summer flowers. Waiters brought delicacies and never let a glass go empty.

Lord Provost sat on my left while London sat on my right. I engaged in conversation about the general happenings in Scotland. He asked me about Stirling Castle, and I gave him a polite answer. His wife sat beside him, beautiful but clearly bored.

Dinner was served, and the quiet conversations continued.

London ate everything on her plate even though she hardly ever had much of an appetite. She never asked what anything was even though it probably wasn't obvious to a foreigner. She did her best to be as respectful as possible, even though she was trapped at my side.

The First Minister took to the stage and began the award

ceremony, recognizing Scottish citizens for their contributions to the territory, as well as the United Kingdom as a whole. They listed off a few names, one man serving in the military, and another for her social work at an orphanage.

And then they called my name.

"The Duke of Rothesay. For excellence in preserving history and tradition, the scotch created in this glorious country continues to give Scotland its fine name. In addition to his founding and continued support of Aberlour Child Care Trust."

The audience erupted in applause, and I rose from my seat, catching a glimpse of the shocked expression on London's face, and then walked to the front to be kissed by the queen and receive my award. Photographers took our picture before I returned to my seat.

London still looked shocked. "Did you know?"

I nodded then sipped my wine.

"Why didn't you tell me?" she whispered.

"Because I wanted to see the look on your face—and I did."

18

LONDON

As the night progressed, we were moved inside the palace for dessert and wine. Men lit up cigars, and people spoke quietly together, the mingling continuing. Even though I knew the date, it seemed like I had stepped back in time to another era. I was standing among monarchs whose blood ran deep into history.

Including my date.

Crewe was social as he chatted with people he'd known since childhood, princes from distant lands and monarchs from other countries. His hand was usually around my waist, keeping me close to his side like I might drift away.

We moved away and approached the dessert table, the

decadent sweets appeared almost fake because they looked so good. I wanted to try one of the brownies, but I was terrified of getting anything on my dress. Normally, I wouldn't care. But this gown cost a fortune, and I didn't want to embarrass myself in front of these noble people.

"Are you going to get anything?" Crewe asked quietly, standing beside me.

"I want to but…" My hand moved to my stomach. "I shouldn't."

He rolled his eyes. "You're drop-dead gorgeous, and you know it. You can eat everything on this table and still be the most beautiful woman in this room."

His compliment swept through my entire body, making me feel warmth that had nothing to do with the wine. "I'm just afraid I'll stain my dress…"

"Oh…" He smirked and covered it as he drank his wine. "Well, yeah. You better not do that."

I had the strength to turn away from the delicious morsels, but I secretly knew I would regret not trying everything at this dinner. "I have to ask you something."

"Great," he said with a sigh. "I knew the questions would start eventually."

"You sell intelligence to people, right?"

His eyes darkened at the topic. "Yes. It's one of my many businesses."

"So, you mingle with all these monarchs like you're friends and then turn around and sell their secrets for cash? Correct me if I'm wrong, but you seem rich enough to not have to resort to such betrayal." I couldn't keep the accusation out of my tone. Sometimes he did thoughtful things that surprised me, and then I remembered he did unforgivable things too.

"You're right, for the most part."

"Why would you do such a thing?"

He didn't even bother to pretend to look guilty. "I have my reasons."

"There's a reason besides money?"

He discreetly glanced around to make sure no one was eavesdropping on us. "I don't sell intelligence from my allies. That would be treason."

My eyebrows narrowed in confusion. "I don't understand..."

He turned his back to the rest of the room, giving us more

privacy. He lowered his voice as he spoke. "A lot of these officials have information about other parts of the world, from threatening countries. I extract that information and sell it to the highest bidder."

While I was still confused, that didn't sound nearly as bad as I initially thought. "And what's the point of all this?"

He brought his wine to his lips and took a drink. "You take down leaders without declaring war."

This had to be about more than just money. It seemed like a lot of work for a rich man of royalty. "There's something you aren't telling me."

His eyes softened as he looked into mine. "As a member of Scottish royalty, I can't directly do anything against the men I despise. If I did, it could be considered an act of war from the United Kingdom. The queen is a very peaceful person and has already lived through one great war. I doubt she wants to live through another." He took another drink, his eyes dark with simmering aggression.

"So you're basically selling intelligence to men who have a common enemy?"

He nodded. "Exactly."

"And you're making money off it at the same time?"

He nodded again. "You're bright and beautiful."

The compliment washed over me without seeping into my skin because I was too invested in the conversation to care about anything else. "Who is your enemy and why?" It was a personal question, but since I'd been sleeping with him for two months, I had the right to ask.

He inserted one hand into his pocket and glanced around to make sure no one was looking. "Russia. Not the people but the leaders. Secretary-General, Boris Peskov, was responsible for the death of my parents, and later, my older brother, Alec."

I'd wondered about his family halfway through dinner. If they were alive, they would have been there, so I already made the assumption they were dead. I didn't realize their death was caused by an international breach of code. "I...I'm sorry." I actually felt pity in my heart, instantly sad for this man who kept me as a prisoner against my will. When he hurt, I hurt too. He didn't deserve an ounce of my sympathy, but yet, he had it. I moved into his chest and wrapped my arms around his neck, holding him because that was all I knew how to do.

He stiffened at the touch then wrapped his arms around my waist. He rested his chin on my head and took a deep breath, his powerful chest expanding against my cheek. "It was a long time ago."

When I pulled away, I stood on my tiptoes and gave him a quick kiss. Our soft mouths pressed together, both tasting like wine and scotch. I stepped back, knowing I shouldn't give him too much affection in a public place like this.

He stared at me blankly, like he could hardly believe what I just did.

"What happened?" I finally asked.

He stared at me for a few more minutes, his brown eyes soft like melted chocolate. He set his glass down on an empty tray a waiter carried as he passed, and then Crewe inserted his other hand into his pocket. "My father was a duke as well as a diplomat, so they traveled to Russia to discuss an international children's program. During transfer from the airport to the palace, a lone gunman fired into their car and shot both of my parents. Alec survived and was rescued by Russian police. But he mysteriously fell ill during transport and died before he returned home. At the time, I was very young, so I stayed in Glasgow with Finley. I was just six at the time."

I didn't know what to say. The story was appalling and

devastating. One day, his family left and never returned home. "Did they ever figure out who the gunman was?"

Crewe shook his head. "No. I think the Secretary-General of Russia was behind it."

"That's quite an accusation…"

"I have my reasons," he said quietly. "I found out he used to be in love with my mother. He pursued her, but she denied his advances. Then she married my father, someone with more money and power. I suspect he never got over the rejection. So he murdered all of them, including her oldest son." He said everything without an ounce of emotion, like this wasn't his own family he was discussing.

"The queen never moved against them?"

"Russia is a terrifying country. Without any evidence, there was nothing we could do. The public was angry for the first year, but eventually, people moved on with their lives. Obviously, I never have. So I encourage Russian enemies to do the dirty work for me."

I wasn't expecting such an extravagant tale. It was mind-boggling and heartbreaking at the same time. "I'm sorry. I know I said that already, but I mean it…"

"I know." He moved his hand to my chest and brushed his fingers against my soft skin. He watched my lips for a moment like he might kiss me, but then he thought better of it. He lowered his hand. "He'll get what's coming to him eventually."

"So, Finley raised you?" Now it made sense why they were so close.

"For the most part. He's been part of the family for a very long time."

"Do you have any other family?"

Crewe shook his head. "I'm the last of the bloodline."

"That means you need to have children."

He nodded. "I do."

That meant he would let me go eventually. Obviously, I couldn't be his wife and give him children. He would have to marry a duchess or a princess or something, not some American woman.

We stared at each other in silence, the sadness hanging in the air between us. I lost my family far too early in life, but he lost his even earlier. My parents weren't murdered, but we still had a lot in common. "I'm going to use the restroom. Do you know which way it is?" I wanted a moment to compose myself, to really think about what he just said.

His hand moved to my waist, and he nodded to the hallway. "Down and to the left."

"Thank you."

He placed a kiss on my temple before he released me, my body feeling warm at the unexpected touch. The second his hand released me, I felt the sting of the cold. He gave me a final look before he walked away, his shoulders broad and powerful. He commanded the room with just his silence, his kingly grace.

My eyes were transfixed before I finally turned away and followed his directions. I entered the hallway and turned to the left. A man stood there in a waiter's uniform, but he didn't contain a tray. His eyes honed in on me like he recognized me, but I didn't have a clue who he was so there was no way I was familiar to him.

He stepped in my way, his hand behind his back. "London Ingram?"

How did he know my name? "Yes?"

"Please come with me."

"Where?" I demanded. "Why?"

"Just follow me." He walked down the hallway and turned right, away from the bathroom.

My body told me this wasn't a good idea, that I could be walking into some kind of trap. But my gut told me to follow because he would lead me somewhere I was meant to be. We were under the queen's protection, and Crewe was just a room away. If anyone could help me, it would be him.

So I followed.

I walked up the stairs and reached the second landing, which was absolutely silent. The sounds of the merriment from the party drifted to my ears, and my dress trailed across the hardwood floor underneath my heels.

He kept going. "This way." He reached the fifth door on the left, checked the hallway to make sure no one was watching, and then opened it. "Go inside. We don't have much time."

"Who are you?"

"Just go." He held the door open.

My arms were covered with bumps, and sweat formed on my temple. My heart was beating so fast it hurt. I tried to steady my breath and remain calm as I walked inside, unsure what I would find waiting for me.

A man in all black stood with his back to me, his hands in his pockets as he stared out the window.

I stared at him, recognizing the soft brown hair that was similar to mine. His posture was familiar, the way he shifted his weight to one foot. The build of his arms reminded me of someone I'd known all my life.

The waiter shut the door, leaving us alone together.

Joseph turned around and stared at me, his eyes taking me in like he hadn't seen me in twenty years. He wasn't an emotional man, usually teasing me rather than paying me a single compliment. But the moment he looked at me, the sadness took up his entire body. "London..." He closed the distance between us and hugged me, holding me so tight it didn't seem like he wanted to let me go. "I'm so sorry..."

I held on to my brother, recognizing his cologne instantly. The last time I saw him on his feet, he had come to the city for Christmas. It was just the two of us in my cramped apartment while the snow fell outside. My radiator was broken, so we spent an entire day freezing until he managed to fix it. At the time, it was terrible. But now it was a cherished memory.

He pulled away, the same sadness in his eyes. "I don't have a lot of time."

"How did you get in here?"

"We don't have time for that either," he said quietly. "I need to get to the point, London. Crewe is a paranoid man."

"Do you have a plan?"

He nodded. "But you aren't going to like it."

"Do you want me to destroy the detonator. I know he keeps it on him most of the time. I don't know where he puts it when he sleeps…" But if I did enough digging, I could figure it out. He couldn't keep it from me forever.

"That won't work," he said. "Even if you recover it, he'll have a way of overriding it."

"You think?"

"Definitely. Crewe always covers his tracks. He's not a guy you fuck with."

But yet, you did. "So you're saying there's nothing we can do? We aren't even going to try?"

"There's only one way out of this. And it's not a plan either of us will like."

He was going to ask me to kill Crewe. There was no other way. But the idea of ending his life, stabbing a knife through his heart, brought me nothing but pain. I had every right to do whatever was necessary to save both myself and my brother, but I couldn't bring myself to do that. Despite what he'd done to both of us, I didn't want to hurt Crewe.

"You have to get him to fall in love with you."

I stared at him blankly, unsure if he really said those words. "Are you insane? That's never going to happen. I thought you were going to ask me to kill him."

"That would never work," he said. "Crewe is too smart for that."

"And he's too hollow to feel anything real for anyone—especially me." Crewe had a line of beautiful women at his beck and call. He could be with princesses and foreign diplomats. He could go to Milan and find a model. There was no way I would ever be enough to keep him around.

"I don't believe that. He took you to one of the biggest social events of the year. He could have taken anyone, but he chose you."

"That doesn't mean anything." I had to admit it was odd to bring some boring American girl. But I couldn't read too much into it.

"We both know you're smart, witty, and beautiful." It was the first time Joseph paid me a real compliment. "The guy would be an idiot not to feel something for you. You're charming and a smartass—in a good way."

Since we were in a rush, I didn't have time to even crack a smile. "I seriously don't think that's going to work. We have to think of something else."

"Just be whatever he wants you to be. Be whatever fantasy he likes. Say the things he wants to hear."

Easier said than done.

"The only way he's gonna give up that detonator is if he actually starts caring about you. Otherwise, he's going to hold it over both of our heads for the rest of our lives. It's the only way out for both of us."

I was willing to do anything to free my brother, even something as sinister as this. I didn't think it was likely to succeed, but I had to try if there was no other alternative. "I'll do my best…"

"Thanks." His eyes filled with clouds as the silence

stretched between us. He put his hands in his pockets and cleared his throat. "Does he treat you well?" Joseph cringed like he didn't want to truly hear the answer.

Even if he didn't, I would have lied about it. "Yeah, he does."

"Really?" he whispered.

I nodded. "It could be a lot worse. He doesn't hurt me."

Joseph suddenly looked away like he was ashamed of the thoughts in his mind. He was probably thinking about the things Crewe did to me at night when we were in bed together. Ashamed that he couldn't save me, he couldn't look at me.

"He's not as bad as he seems." I wasn't just saying this to make Joseph feel better. It was the truth. "He doesn't let the other men touch me. He gives me everything I need. And he protects me against everything. We have dinner together and talk. I would much rather be with him than go to Bones…" That man was utterly terrifying. I wouldn't be alive right now if I'd been transferred into his care. "I think there's a chance he could be a good guy underneath all that darkness…"

Joseph looked up, meeting my gaze. "It sounds like you like him."

"No," I said quickly. "I just think there's hope." Now that I knew he'd lost so much at such a young age, I understood his need for power and control. When he was vulnerable and young, there was nothing he could do to protect his family. He had to wait years before he was even big enough to do anything about it. By the time he was an adult, they'd been gone for twelve years. Now he had to make a name for himself, to be as threatening and terrifying as possible.

I understood him a lot better now.

"I'll get in contact with you again," he said. "I don't know when or how. But I'll figure it out."

"Okay."

He sighed when he knew this was goodbye. "I'm so sorry I got you into this."

"It's okay." He shouldn't be working in this kind of business, and he certainly shouldn't have robbed a man of four million dollars. But the time for a lecture had passed. He'd already learned his lesson.

"I would do anything to change places with you."

"I know, Joey."

He pulled me in for another hug. "You should get going…he'll start to get suspicious."

"I know." I didn't want to let go of my brother just yet. He felt like home.

For the first time ever, he kissed me on the head. "We'll figure this out. I promise."

"I know."

He pulled away, reluctant.

Tears pooled in my eyes, but I fought them back. If Crewe saw them, he would ask a million questions. I didn't want him to figure out what had happened here. And I didn't want him to hit the trigger on that detonator. "I'll see you later."

Joseph gave a quick nod.

I walked out without looking back, knowing I would start to cry if I saw the devastation on my brother's face. The guilt he carried because of my imprisonment was killing him. I could see it in his limbs as well as his face. I walked down the stairs then returned to the drawing room where everyone was still mingling.

I spotted Crewe against the wall near the window. He was speaking with a beautiful woman with brown hair, wearing a champagne pink dress that complimented her dark skin. She was naturally radiant, looking like a princess without a tiara. She stood close to Crewe like she knew him well, and then her hand moved to his wrist.

As I approached them, I felt the blood pound in my ears. Her blue eyes were glued to Crewe's like he was the only person in the entire room. She watched his lips as he spoke, hanging on to every word like she was afraid she would miss something.

Now I started to feel angry, wondering what was going on right under my nose. Was she one of the women he slept with on a regular basis? Was this a former lover? A current lover? The second I went to the bathroom, he was already flirting with someone else? If that was the case, the plan would never succeed.

I finally reached Crewe, standing so close to him that it was unmistakable I was his date—not her. I gave her a fake smile, just to make sure I wasn't offending a monarch who could get me thrown out of this place.

Crewe turned to me when he realized I was there. He didn't change his posture or look alarmed like he'd been caught doing something wrong. "Hello, Lovely." He greeted me with a slight smile but didn't touch me.

The nickname wasn't enough affection for me. I grabbed his hand and interlocked our fingers. It was the first time we'd held hands this way. It was juvenile affection, something young lovers did. But I wasn't going to stand there and let this woman think Crewe was available.

Crewe stared at our joined hands but didn't make a comment. "Allow me to introduce you to Josephine, The Duchess of Cambridge."

I gave a slight bow, still wearing a forced smile.

"And this is London." Crewe didn't refer to me in any possessive manner. But there wasn't a realistic title to explain what I was to him. Prisoner? I doubt that would go over well with the duchess.

She wore a smile faker than mine. "Pleasure to meet you. Please excuse me." She walked away, her pink gown moving across the floor. She held her shoulders so far back that her chest looked even more robust. Diamond earrings hung in her lobes, sparkling under the light of the chandeliers. She looked more graceful than the queen herself.

When she was gone, Crewe took his hand away from mine. He placed it around my waist instead. That arrogant smile stretched his lips, and I already knew what he was going to say before he even said it. "You know, it kinda seemed like you were jealous for a moment there."

I stared him down, not finding his words remotely comical. "I was."

He was about to chuckle but stopped himself when he heard what I said. He nearly did a double take, surprised by my confession.

"I saw the way she looked at you."

Crewe's eyes darkened, his eyebrows slightly furrowing.

"What is she to you? Were you once together?"

Crewe didn't answer my question. "That's none of your concern."

That was enough of an answer for me. "Is it over?"

"I'm here with you, aren't I?"

That didn't answer my question. "I want to be the only woman in your bed."

His eyes narrowed again. "For a prisoner, you sure seem to like me."

He was a playboy, a dictator, and an asshole. It would be tough work to make this man fall for me, let alone simply care about me. But Joseph was right. Pulling his heartstrings like he was a puppet would be the only way out of this mess. "Is it really so much to ask for your fidelity?" I wouldn't be able to manipulate him if he was getting action everywhere else.

"It's too much to ask for anything. I'm in charge here. Don't forget it."

I grabbed him by the tie and pulled his mouth to mine, giving him a kiss that was a little too rough for such a public place.

But he didn't stop the kiss.

I was the first one to pull away, to feel the swelling of my lips.

He stared at me hard, his brown eyes trained on my expression. He looked like he wanted to pick me up and pin me against the wall, fucking me then and there. "We'll pick this up when we get home."

"No." I released his tie and smoothed it out over his chest. "We'll pick this up in the car."

19

CREWE

I thought I would enjoy the hurt look on Josephine's face.

But I didn't.

Actually, I didn't care at all.

Slowly, the blood drained from her face, and her cheeks turned pale. Her eyes lost their innate sparkle, something I'd come to notice since I knew her so well. The second she laid eyes on London and saw our fingers intertwined together, she knew I'd moved on.

And it broke her heart.

Too bad, so sad.

After we said our goodbyes, we returned to the

roundabout entryway and waited for my driver to arrive. All I wanted to do was return to the castle so I could rip that expensive gown off London and fuck her until dawn. I liked the possessiveness she showed, although I couldn't explain why. She was definitely mine, but I would never be hers. She wanted me to be monogamous with her, and I was, but I refused to tell her that. She would know she had some kind of control over me.

I couldn't allow that.

I would much rather her think I was out fucking around every time I wasn't in her presence than let her know she was enough to satisfy me. The greatest kings had been destroyed by the greatest women. Men were the ones who ruled the world, but in reality, the world was ruled by the women who ruled the men.

I wouldn't let that happen to me.

It didn't matter how fond I'd grown of London. It didn't matter that I actually respected her. It didn't matter that I didn't mean a word I said when I threatened to kill her brother. There were lines I refused to cross.

The car arrived and Dunbar opened the door to the back seat. I allowed London to enter first before I got in behind her. The windows in the back were tinted to the darkest shade, and the visor between Dunbar and me was closed once I pressed my finger to the button. He already knew where he was going so I didn't need to say a word to him.

We pulled onto the main road and London crawled into my lap and straddled my hips. Her enormous gown stretched across the seat and the floor, ruffling at every move she made. Her hands dug into my hair, and she kissed me hard on the mouth, devouring me like she'd been wanting to have me all night.

I didn't like being on the bottom. I didn't like surprises. I didn't like letting someone take over.

But I thought it was pretty hot with London.

I moved my hands up her dress and touched her smooth thighs, my cock hard in my slacks and pressed against her panties. I gripped her ass with my strong hands and slowly grinded against her, rubbing against her sensitive clit the way she liked.

She panted into my mouth, her fingers digging into my shoulders.

All thoughts of Josephine were gone. London was the only woman I thought about.

She continued kissing me, undoing my slacks and

yanking down my boxers so my cock could appear. She pulled her thong over then slowly lowered herself onto my length. Her lips stopped moving against my mouth as she took in the inches that stretched her wide apart. A quiet moan escaped her lips, enjoying my steel rod.

When she had every inch, she sat in my lap and hooked her arms around my neck. The car drove down the road, changing lanes from time to time. The sounds of traffic could be heard, and every now and then, a honk.

My fingers moved to the buttons mounted on the ceiling, and I hit the radio. Classical musical filled the backseat of the car. I didn't want Dunbar to hear how sexy London sounded when she came, her beautiful moans echoing in the car. He would beat off to it later, and that was something I couldn't allow.

Only I beat off to her.

She breathed hard as she rode me, taking in my length over and over. She rocked her hips the way I taught her, grinding her clit against my pelvic bone. She threw her head back then pulled down the front of her dress so her tits could come out. Then she began to play with them, her hips still rolling.

Fuck.

I pressed my face into the valley of her breasts and inhaled her beautiful scent. My tongue moved along her skin and tasted her sweetness. My cock continued to pound into her, feeling that wetness that greeted me since the first time I fucked her. This woman wanted me at all times. She was the best prisoner I'd ever had.

And the only one.

"Your pussy is fucking divine." I pressed my feet against the floor and thrust upward into her, shoving my entire nine inches inside her. There was nowhere else my cock would rather be than inside this smartass beauty.

"I love your cock." Her hands kept playing with her tits as she panted. Her eyes were locked with mine before she threw her head back, her beautiful hair trailing across her shoulders as she moved.

A moan escaped the back of my throat. Her enthusiasm was sexy as hell, and it turned me into a wild animal. All I knew was I needed to fuck her hard and long. I needed to be inside her to survive. Food, water, and protection was negligent. I just needed her.

She dropped her hands from her tits and returned her arms around my waist, her hips still rocking. "I'm already gonna come…" She kissed my neck then nibbled on my lobe, her sexy pants loud and clear.

"Come all over my dick, Lovely." I gripped her ass and pulled her onto my cock harder, wanting to give her a climax that made her toes curl.

"God, yes…" She stopped breathing, her chest expanded with the breath she held. Her nails began to sink through my clothes and directly into my skin. She moved her face to mine and gave me the sexiest look I'd ever seen. Then she exploded, gushing all over my cock. "Crewe…yes…Crewe."

I loved it when she said my name. It really made me feel like a king. I wanted to come, but I wanted to keep going, knowing the drive would last for at least an hour. What better way to pass the time than by fucking an exquisite woman?

Once she came down from her high, I rolled her onto her back on the leather seat, her head resting by the door. Her legs automatically hooked around my waist, and she dug her fingers into my hair again.

I pounded into her, pinning her against the seat and the door. My hips worked, fucking her until she was sore. My cock slid through her overwhelming slickness, and I knew she loved my cock as much as I loved giving it to her.

I was gonna make her come again before we were done.

"Crewe…you feel so good." She kissed the corner of my mouth, a film of sweat over the skin. "I love it when you fuck me hard."

"You haven't seen anything yet, Lovely." My slacks fell below my ass, but I kept working, needing to give it to her hard enough to make her come again.

Now I didn't give a damn if Dunbar heard.

She grabbed my ass and pulled me deep into her, slowing down the strokes to make them long and hard. My body rubbed against her clit again, stimulating the wet nub. "Yes…right there."

I looked into her eyes, ready for the sight. "I'm gonna give it to you…"

"Good. I love it when you fill me…" She spoke with lidded eyes and a sex-crazed expression, looking like the sexiest thing I'd ever seen.

She turned into such a vixen. The sex had always been good, but this was phenomenal. She was dirty, kinky. She wanted my seed deep inside her, to make her feel full. And I wanted to give it to her just as much.

She dragged her nails down my back. "Okay...I'm about to come. I want it, Crewe."

I pressed my forehead to hers and closed my eyes, feeling the powerful explosion sweep over my body. It rushed over me in waves, making me feel both alive and dead at the same time. My cock twitched as it became harder, and then I felt the rush pass through me.

I came with a groan, filling her pussy with as much come as I could give.

Once she felt it, she moaned louder, coming with me. Her pussy guzzled all of it, gushing around me at the exact same time. "Crewe."

"Lovely."

We rode our high together, feeling the pure wonderfulness. Our bodies were slick with sweat and our hair was a mess, but neither one of us cared. We were both satisfied—for now. I kissed her upper lip and kept her pinned underneath me, wanting my cock to remain deep inside as long as possible.

She hooked her ankles together and kept me in place. "Let's stay like this until we get home…"

She read my mind. I shifted her body until we were side by side, my softening cock still inside her. I stared at her beside me, watching her eyes close in exhaustion. Her green eyes were hiding behind her lids, but I watched her soft expression, the way her eyebrows relaxed once she began to drift away. Her makeup hadn't smudged despite the sweat, and her curls remained in place despite how hard I yanked on them. Just as perfect as when we left, she looked beautiful.

Too beautiful.

When I woke up the following morning, London was still beside me. I was usually long gone before she woke up, heading out for a work out or getting down to business. But we were up late last night, so I allowed myself the luxury of sleeping in.

She was on her stomach, her head facing the other way.

I moved on top of her and pressed kisses down her spine, trailing to the top of her ass.

She sighed quietly in her sleep, in the land of dreams.

I hoped I was there too.

I got out of bed and headed downstairs for coffee and breakfast. It was a nice day, so I intended to spend my morning in the courtyard.

"Mr. Donoghue." Dunbar emerged from behind me, coming out of the shadows of the massive castle.

I didn't break my stride, recognizing his voice anyway. "Yes?"

"The Duchess of Cambridge is here to see you."

I stopped in my tracks and turned around, unable to believe my ears. "Josephine is here?"

"I asked her to wait for you in the garden room. Or should I tell her you're busy?"

Not even I would turn away the Duchess of Cambridge. It was beyond rude. "Did she say what she wanted?" After our conversation last night, it didn't seem like there was much left to discuss—especially alone.

"No, sir."

I crossed my arms over my chest then felt the thick stubble across my jaw.

Dunbar patiently waited for me to make a decision.

"Tell her I'll be there in fifteen minutes." That would give me enough time to prepare myself.

"Yes, sir." Dunbar turned around.

"Tell Marcus to prepare breakfast, coffee, and tea for the duchess."

He kept walking. "Absolutely."

I sighed as I thought to myself, suspecting I knew exactly what she wanted to discuss. I quickly darted back upstairs and got ready, brushing my teeth and taking a quick shower. Just when I was about to walk out, London stirred.

"Morning." She sat up, her hair still slightly curly from last night.

I was in a hurry, so I didn't break my stride. "I have a meeting. I'll see you in about an hour."

"It's Sunday. Who works on a Sunday?"

I gave her a cold look. "Me. I work every day." I walked out, annoyed she'd questioned me. I realized she wasn't a staff member so her position was different, but I still didn't like it. I headed downstairs and moved to the garden room on the west side of the castle. I wore slacks and a blue collared shirt, refusing to put on a suit when she dropped by unannounced.

I walked inside, seeing the sunlight filter through the room. The royal furniture had withstood hundreds of years, even though most of it had been refurbished or preserved. She sat in the armchair with her tea cup on the coffee table, steaming and untouched. She wore a bright blue dress, nearly the same color as her eyes. "Your Royal Highness—"

"Please don't call me anything other than Josephine when it's just the two of us." She looked at me with eyes full of despair.

I sat in the other armchair, refusing to greet her with any kind of touch. The room filled with obvious tension, our old relationship eliciting memories for both of us. She stared at me with a look of longing, words practically written on her face.

I wanted this conversation to remain professional. Whatever her intentions were, I didn't want to be caught up in a scandal. "I'm very busy this afternoon, so please get on with it." I didn't stop myself from being rude, but I stopped myself from insulting her.

She sighed before she spoke. "Henry and I are getting married in a month, and I just—"

"Having cold feet is natural. Don't worry about it."

"It's not that..." She scooted closer to the edge of the armchair. She would touch me if she could.

"Then I don't know what to say, Josephine." We weren't friends, so she better not expect me to give her advice. Her personal life was none of my concern. "Henry seems like a nice fellow. You know he's wealthy and has a direct line to the throne. Sounds exactly like something you'd want." I kept the bitterness out of my tone, but only barely.

"I think I made a mistake." She whispered so quietly I could hardly hear her. "Crewe, I don't love him. I thought I could, but I don't. But with you—"

"We're done, Josephine." There was no possibility of us ever having a future together. She humiliated me in front of everyone I know. She turned her back on me when I never turned my back on her.

She winced at the blunt way I silenced her. "I still love you..."

I looked out the window, refusing to meet her gaze. Her words were empty. They didn't mean a damn thing to me.

"Do you still love me, Crewe?"

I rubbed my fingers across my stubble. "No." I didn't feel the sting of regret. I didn't feel the pain. All I felt was nothing. "I've moved on, Josephine. Even if I still felt the same way, I would never go back to you."

"Why?"

I laughed because the question was stupid. "You humiliated me. That's why. You think I'm some imbecile you can play games with? I let my guard down for you, and only you, and you fucking betrayed me. Fuck you, Josephine."

She closed her eyes as if she was about to cry.

"You have a lot of nerve coming here, to my home, and asking me to take you back. Jesus Christ, you're engaged to another man."

"I know but…" The tears began to pour. "When I saw you with her…I knew I made a mistake."

I rolled my eyes. "I've been with a lot of women since you, Josephine."

She flinched as if I had slapped her.

"You should leave before anyone finds out you're here." I rose to my feet, not looking at her. "I mean this in the most respectful way possible, get the hell out and don't come back. You aren't welcome here."

She rose to her feet, the tears falling freely. "I know I hurt you, and I'm sorry for that. I know I made a mistake—"

I stayed by the door so I wouldn't slap her. "It wasn't a fucking mistake. You chose him over me. Plain and simple. You cared more about his wealth and power than settling for the Duke of Rothesay—a man who actually loved you. So enjoy your loveless, passionless marriage to a man who will fuck his concubines every time you're out of the country."

She wiped her tears on the back of her hand and sniffed. "Crewe—"

"Get the fuck out, or I'll drag you out." I walked out of the room, my shoulders bunched and tense. I wanted to punch a hole in the stone and watch the castle crumble down. I wanted to hurt Josephine for everything she'd done to me.

I wanted to break her the way she broke me.

"I don't want you to be like this." Her tearful voice came from behind me. "I don't want you to be this angry."

"Too fucking bad. When someone betrays my trust, that's it. It's gone." I kept walking, heading to the front door so I could get rid of her for good. "And I wouldn't be so angry if I didn't have to look at you right now." I reached the front door and tore it open. "Disappear, Josephine. Don't speak to me again. When we run into each other, pretend you don't know me. Because I'll pretend I don't even remember your name." I grabbed her by the elbow and shoved her through the threshold before I slammed the door.

Once the solid wood was between us, I took a deep breath and controlled my temper. My knuckles still craved to slam into something. My body wanted to demolish the foundations of this castle. I wanted to go back out there and make Josephine understand just how much she ruined me.

I finally turned around, needing to drink this problem away so I wouldn't think about it anymore.

London stood at the bottom of the stairs, wearing leggings and a pink sweater. Her hair was thrown into a bun, and her face was free of makeup. First thing in the morning, she always looked like a flower that had just blossomed. For a second, her beauty made me forget my anger. Her emerald eyes made me forget my pain. Her noticeable curves, even in baggy clothes, made me think about our nights together.

But the sympathy in her eyes fueled me all over again.

I walked away from her, refusing to speak about the conversation she'd just witnessed. I refused to answer the hundreds of questions running through her mind. I refused to answer to anyone but myself.

Josephine had already turned me into a fool—for the whole world to see. I didn't trust anyone because no one was trustworthy. I was always one step ahead of my enemies, intent on making them into the fools. My heart was dead, along with everyone else I cared about. Now all I wanted was revenge for all the things that happened to me.

And one day, I would get it.

20

LONDON

Crewe avoided me all day, hiding out somewhere else in the castle. He didn't join me for meals or conversation. He didn't want me for sex.

I gave him his space for as long as I could. But my curiosity was getting the best of me. His relationship with Josephine was far more serious than I had realized. And she must have done something terrible to him because I'd never seen him that mad.

Not once.

I searched the castle to find him, and eventually found him in the second drawing room on the opposite side of the castle. He was sitting alone, reading a book while his cigar burned in the ashtray and a half bottle of scotch sat beside him.

I crept into the room so he wouldn't notice me. But when I was fifteen feet away, he heard my footsteps and looked up. He watched me with eyes blacker than coal. Nothing about his exterior was welcoming. He threatened me with his silence, commanding me to leave the room or there would be consequences.

"I'm not here to talk." I slowly crept closer, stopping at the chair near the window.

His shoulders relaxed slightly when he heard my declaration.

I moved between his knees then crawled into his lap, pushing the book aside so there was plenty of room.

When he let the book drop to the ground, I knew I was welcome.

I straddled his hips then ran my hands up his chest, feeling the powerful muscle underneath. I looked into his dark eyes and didn't spot the warmth I was accustomed to. I just saw an angry man.

I wanted to know every detail about what happened with his former lover, but he wouldn't give me any answers. I would have to wait for another time or uncover them on my own. But if I had any chance of getting this man to feel something for me, I had to be his confidant, not his interrogator.

I eyed the cigar on the table and grabbed it from the ashtray. I brought it to my lips and inhaled.

His lips softened into a smile.

I pulled the smoke into my lungs but then felt my chest convulse in protest. I turned my head and coughed everything out, feeling my lungs scream from the intrusion.

Crewe chuckled. "Takes practice."

I downed his scotch to clear my throat, and while the liquor burned, it was nothing in comparison to the smoke. "That doesn't even taste good. I don't get it."

"It'll grow on you." He took the cigar out of my hand and inhaled it into his lungs. Then he turned his head and blew it out, like a man in a tobacco ad. He dropped it back into the ashtray. "You finally found me, huh?"

"It took me a while. But I followed the scent of cigars and booze."

He chuckled again. "Led you right to me, I guess."

"Yep." I rubbed his chest again, wanting to feel connected to him.

He leaned his head back and watched me, his eyes taking in my features. Even though I didn't ask a single question, he addressed my curiosity. "I don't want to discuss it, so don't bother asking."

"I wasn't going to ask. I know you better than that."

His eyes didn't soften, but his body relaxed.

I massaged his shoulders, feeling the tension. "So, what now?"

"I don't understand your question, Lovely."

When he used my nickname, I knew he was in a better mood. "Are we staying here? Going back to Fair Isle?"

"We're going to Italy," he said matter-of-factly.

"What's there?"

"I have a friend who lives in Tuscany. Crow Barsetti. He usually has good information that I in turn sell."

"Does he charge you for this?"

"No. I'm one of his biggest customers."

"What does he sell?" I would never keep track of all these things.

"Weapons."

It's probably where all Crewe's men got their guns and ammo, not to mention, the weapons Crewe used himself.

"It's beautiful there. I think you'll appreciate it."

"I've never been, so I'm sure I will."

He took another drag of his cigar then stood up, lifting me with him. He carried me to the wall then pressed me up against it. One hand undid his slacks and pulled out his cock before he lifted up my dress and pulled my thong to the side. Then he shoved himself violently within me.

"Oh yes…" My arms used his shoulders as an anchor to move myself up and down, taking his cock as he gave it to me. It felt so good that I didn't need to put on a show. He was better than any man I'd ever had. In fact, he made the others look like boys.

He pressed his mouth to my ear, giving me his warm breaths. "I'm going to fuck you all over the world, Lovely."

Instead of sounding alarming, that sounded appealing. "Please do."

I didn't have much to pack, just my clothes and some jewelry. I didn't have much to my name. In fact, I didn't even have my freedom. Lately, my lack of independence didn't feel so daunting, but nonetheless, it was there.

Crewe walked into the room wearing dark jeans and a black t-shirt. His arms looked muscular, perfect for gripping, and his ass was tight, as usual. "Ready, Lovely?"

I looked at my two suitcases. It was everything I owned. "Yeah." I sat on the foot of the bed and pulled my knees to my chest.

He grabbed one of his bags and handed it off to Dunbar outside the door. When he came back to me, he gave me a concerned look. "Everything alright?"

"Yeah, I'm just tired." I thought about Joseph and the last time I saw him. He was on the verge of tears, which was saying something since he was one of the manliest men I knew. He didn't show emotion often—if ever. He was still worried about me, hoping I could accomplish what we agreed to do.

But now that I witnessed Crewe's fight with Josephine, I didn't think it was possible.

Crewe was cut off from the world for a reason. He didn't trust anyone for a reason. He had to exert his control and power over everything—for a reason. He'd lost more than he could afford, and the woman he obviously cared for had betrayed him in some way.

How could I get someone so scarred to let me in? Especially when it was just a ploy.

Crewe sat on the bed beside me and looked at me. "You know you can talk to me, right?"

"Yes. You can talk to me too."

"It just seems like something is bothering you." He never asked about my feelings before. Maybe we were making more progress than I realized.

"I guess I miss home… I miss my brother."

His expression didn't change, showing no sympathy.

"I miss the humidity of New York. I miss the greasy Chinese food."

"Tuscany is very humid. But you won't find any Chinese food there." He gave me a smile, trying to cheer me up.

"I'm sure the Italian food will be great, so it'll be alright." I looked at the royal chambers one last time, feeling a little sad to leave it behind. It really was a beautiful place. It contained more history than a text book.

He patted my thigh before he rose to his feet. "I'll be downstairs when you're ready." He grabbed my bags and walked out, meeting Dunbar in the hallway.

I stayed behind and enjoyed the solitude, thinking of the path laid out before me. I needed to crack down on my mission, to learn as much as I could about the man who kept me as a prisoner. I needed to learn his strengths as well as his weaknesses.

And I needed to learn how to make him fall in love with me.

London's story continues in The Scotch Queen, available now.

Order Now

ABOUT THE AUTHOR

KEEP IN TOUCH WITH PENELOPE

Subscribe to my newsletter for updates on new releases and giveaways.

Sign up today.

www.PenelopeSky.com

penelopeskybooks@gmail.com

78711163R00191

Made in the USA
Lexington, KY
12 January 2018